Skirt Chaser

(Book one of the Confessions of a Chick Magnet series)

by Jenny Gardiner

Copyright © 2018 by Jenny Gardiner
Cover art by Kim Killion, The Killion Group, Inc.
ISBN-13: 978-1944763237

What people are saying about Jenny Gardiner's books:

Red Hot Romeo
"Awesome". So enjoyed the romantic chemistry between the two characters. Read it non stop into the wee hours. Highly recommend this book
-- Mrs. K

Blue-Blooded Romeo
"Another brilliant, fun read from Jenny Gardiner. The book is fun to read and I thoroughly enjoyed every word. Jenny Gardiner has put the fun back into romance books and I look forward to each book in this delightful series."
-- Anne Blyth

"I had planned on only reading a few chapters at first but couldn't put it down. A terrific storyline, well-developed and extremely relatable characters, what's not to love?? Great read!"
-- Samantha Reeves

Big O Romeo
"I could not put this book down. Warning don't start this book late at night as you will not want to stop reading.
-- Di

Sleeping with Ward Cleaver

"A fun, sassy read! A cross between Erma Bombeck and Candace Bushnell, reading Jenny Gardiner is like sinking your teeth into a chocolate cupcake...you just want more."

--Meg Cabot, NY Times bestselling author of Princess Diaries, Queen of Babble and more

Slim to None

"Jenny Gardiner has done it again--this fun, fast-paced book is a great summer read."

--Sarah Pekkanen, NY Times bestselling author of *The Opposite of Me*

Chapter One

Twenty Years Earlier

TANNER Eliasson was a lonely boy. The only child of coquettish film star Gina LeFevre and legendary director Brady Cox, he generally came as an afterthought to his busy and self-absorbed parents. Particularly to his father, who was old enough to be his grandfather and never seemed to express much interest in Tanner except to impart annoying aphorisms that he must have fancied were the sage words of wisdom dispensed on high from an elder but instead came across as judgmental insults.

"Man up, son," he'd say if Tanner complained pretty much about anything. "If your only tool is a hammer, every problem looks like a nail."

Tanner didn't even know what the fuck that meant, but he chalked it up to his father being an old man with nothing better to say to a little kid.

His mother, well, the best Tanner could tell, wanted at least to appear to be a loving mother, but the one his mother loved the most was herself. And boy, was she good at that. Unless Tanner wanted to spend an inordinate amount of time with his mother and her vast staff of primpers and fawners—usually spearheaded by her stylist, Eliza Fink and her personal trainer, Jackson Mandelay, oh and her publicist, Orion Something-or-Other (Tanner could never recall her actual name, but it was the best he could remember)—he didn't get much "me time" with his mom.

Because she was always prepping for something, be it a role or an audition for a role or an awards ceremony or her body or an awards ceremony. A whole lotta prepping always going on. He learned early on that it took a lot of time out of your day to be beautiful, and his mother was indeed stunning.

Tall, statuesque, and blond, she often said she was at least pleased that she passed on her half-French, half-Scandinavian beauty to her only child. Daily she would stroke his flaxen locks and remark on how handsome he was, with his sparkling blue eyes, thanks to her. He grew to be embarrassed by his looks. It felt like his mother was complimenting herself when she praised him. Besides, he wanted to be appreciated for who he was, not how he looked.

Tanner didn't spend much time with his folks, but he also didn't spend much time with much of anyone but himself, with the exception of his beloved yellow Labrador, Sunshine, who truly was a ray of sunshine in his world. He knew from the endless gushing of strangers that he lived a charmed life. Outsiders looking in were inherently jealous of his world, what with the Hollywood Hills mansion he lived in, complete with retractable glass walls that overlooked all of Los Angeles, capped off with an infinity pool the color of twilight, built right into the cliff. Sure, by all outward appearances, it looked like a great place to live. But the mansion was enormous and lacking in soul, especially since he was often there alone with his parents' household staff.

Worse still, he lived far from the few peers he had from school. And his parents were never around to take him to playdates. His folks both had drivers, but they were driving *them* places, not him. And that cliff thing? He lost a pet iguana over the side of the pool deck one day, never to be seen again, so there was no charm in teetering on the edge of infinity if it meant your pets died on you with one false move.

When his father was home, he tended to lock himself inside his office and would holler at Tanner if he disturbed his "creative genius." What kind of father would say that? For the most part, his mother was on location, but if not there, she was at the gym or some designer's studio having a fitting for another big event.

Occasionally things livened up at his house. His parents were known to throw raucous parties. Sometimes his mother's actress friends would bring their kids along, so then Tanner would be thrown in with a relative stranger and told to entertain him but always warned to stay away from the swimming pool where the grown-ups were. The kids would usually go down to the home theater and watch cartoons for a while. Then they'd move on to the kitchen to see if Cook could whip up some dinner for them. They sure didn't want to eat the weird food the guests were served. But the caterers would shoo them away, muttering about them being underfoot.

Once his parents' friends Alexa and Armando Lipari showed up at a party with their daughter, Zoey Richards. In Hollywood, lots of kids of celebrities didn't share their parents' names since their folks had to take on stage names to sound more exotic. Zoey was a scrawny, tomboy-looking thing with a pair of dirt-stained jeans full of holes at the knees and long, brown hair that hung halfway down her back. She had huge brown, soulful eyes that seemed to take up half her face, like a kinkajou, a cute little creature his friend Adam kept as a pet. Without so much as a formal introduction, her parents dumped the girl at Tanner's bedroom door with instructions to keep her entertained. Tanner rolled his eyes. What did a ten-year-old boy do with a nine-year-old girl? Ugh.

"I don't know what you like to do," he said with a shrug. "I've got some Legos. Or we can watch TV. Maybe the caterers will be serving something that's not disgusting and we can mooch some of it."

She walked over to the dog sitting on the floor near the bed and sat down to pet it.

"I like your dog." She stroked her ears as she spoke. "What's her name?"

"Sunshine," he said.

She looked skyward as if lost in thought. "That's a good name. She seems cheery."

"Yeah, well, she is."

She frowned, got up off the ground, then hopped onto his bed, swinging her legs as she spoke. "I want to swim."

Tanner shook his head. "Oh, no," he said. "My parents would freak if we went to the pool. I've been told I'm not to bring anyone out to the pool during these parties, so I don't."

She furrowed her brow. "Do you always listen to what your parents tell you to do?"

Tanner thought about it for a minute. Weirdly, yeah. It seemed to be what he did. Maybe because they were rarely around, so it's not like there were a ton of rules, and why not honor the few they had? If they were out of town, he kind of wandered the house and ate potato chips for dinner or went to bed when he wanted to. A driver would show up to take him to school, and another driver would magically appear to bring him back home at the end of the day. Every now and then, he'd get a call from one of his parents—usually his mom—and the call was always placed by her assistant.

"Hold for your mother," Eliza would say.

Then his mom would get on the phone while fielding a few other conversations in the background. She'd make a few loud smooching sounds and say she loved him, then hang up. Sometimes Tanner felt like he was living a movie scene of a life instead of a real one.

"I guess I do what my parents tell me to do," he said, frowning. "Don't you?"

She rolled her eyes. "Please. My parents hardly set the example of how one should behave in the world anyhow. Between the two of them they've had at least three lovers in the past two years, all of whom come and go as if they're our roommates. My mother's latest, some personal trainer named Giorgio, comes down to breakfast in his underwear. I'm pretty sure my father is sleeping with our cleaning lady's daughter. Every time she's at the house, his hands are all over her body."

Tanner could hardly believe what he was hearing. How could a girl her age even know of such things? Granted, kids in Hollywood tended to grow up faster than your average kid, in, say, Milwaukee. But geez, he wouldn't have a clue if his parents were doing things like that.

"C'mon," she said, hopping off the bed and reaching for his hands. "Let's sneak into the pool."

"I'm telling you, we'll get in trouble."

She grinned. She had a nice smile, with cute dimples that punctuated the corners of her mouth. "Trouble is my middle name."

Tanner heaved a deep sigh and relented. Somehow he knew this girl was not going to take no for an answer.

He led her down a back flight of steps, then down a long corridor that bypassed the more public areas of the house.

He didn't want to run into his parents who might put a stop to their plans.

"Do you have a swimsuit?" he asked her.

She shook her head. "I'll swim in my clothes."

"Really? Won't you be uncomfortable?"

"My motto is get comfortable with being uncomfortable."

Tanner thought that was a weird thing for the child of film stars to say. He figured that like him, the one thing she could count on with regularity was being as comfortable as possible. At least physically, if not emotionally. Besides, what an odd girl she was—a proud troublemaker who already had a motto. He tried to think what his motto would be if he were clever enough to come up with one, and the only thing he could imagine was "stay under the radar," which wasn't much of a motto to be proud of. The mean boys at school would probably call him chickenshit for that.

They slipped down a flight of steps used mostly by the household staff and out a back door into the warm night air. Loud squeals and giggles echoed from the back of the house.

"There's no way they're not going to notice us," Tanner said, frowning. He hated to defy his parents. At the very least his father would lecture him about his irresponsible failure to listen to directions.

"Look," Zoey said. "Can you hear the crowd out there? There have to be at least a hundred people. You think anyone's going to notice us? And if they do, it's not like we'll run into our parents. It'll be some strangers we don't even know. It'll be fine." She swatted at his arm. "Live a little. Have some adventure."

They turned the corner and suddenly Tanner grabbed Zoey's wrist and pulled her behind the stately, manicured hedges, where they both peeked over the side of the bush to see what was going on. He gasped loudly and immediately rushed to put his hands over her eyes.

"What the hell are you doing?" She flailed against his hands, which were pressed firmly against her face. "Let go!" She used all of her fingers to peel one of his hands away from her eye.

But by then Tanner had been rendered both speechless and motionless.

"Oh my God," Zoey said, her mouth opened wide as she pointed at what was in front of them: a thicket of men and women—there had to have been at least fifty or so—completely naked. Some milled about, others were engaged in conversation, and others, still, were doing things with one another that Tanner had to assume even the street-smart Zoey couldn't comprehend.

The two of them stood stock-still, mouths agape, as they watched what Tanner would eventually learn was known as an orgy unfold before their eyes. The two of them nearly screamed in shock when they saw their parents pairing off with people who were decidedly not their partners.

It took a few minutes for Tanner to regain his composure, but quickly, he reached for Zoey and grabbed her hand, pulling her toward the house. Luckily she complied, and they practically stampeded over one another to get far, far away from whatever it was those very naked, very noisy, and very creepy people were doing.

"If you ever let one person know about this, I'll never speak to you again," Tanner said, out of breath from running up the stairs so quickly.

"Fine," Zoey said. "Because I never want to see you or your parents or this stupid house ever again." She stormed out of the bedroom and sat in the hallway the rest of the night, refusing to discuss anything. When her parents came for her, she was asleep in front of his door and they asked no questions, which was fine by him.

He could barely believe what he'd seen, and the last thing he wanted to ever do was discuss it again. Thank goodness he wasn't going to have to be around that pushy Zoey Richards ever again too.

Chapter Two

Twenty Years Earlier

ZOEY never quite felt like she fit into her parents' world. They were all glamour and drama and paparazzi flashbulbs. She was more swing-from-the-monkey-bars-and-fall-off-and-break-a-wrist, or better yet scale the ridiculously tall fence that surrounded their imposing Malibu mansion and scrabble down the rocks to the beach, far below. Their world had never interested her.

And after the horrible night at that kid Tanner's place, God, she wanted nothing to do with her parents. Whatever they were taking part in was not something she wanted to know about. Seeing those men with those things sticking out from between their legs about made her die. And the women, with freakishly huge boobs that looked like Macy's Thanksgiving Day Parade floats. Yeesh. Her chest was as flat as an ironing board so she couldn't relate to that and honestly, those things scared her. If she ever grew something like them, she'd seek medical assistance to get rid of 'em. That night, it was as if they'd walked in on some Monster's Ball. Only at least the monsters would probably be covered in fur or something. Not naked with those icky things sticking out. Yuck. A good month had passed since then, and still, it made her sick to her stomach to think about that night.

Tonight her folks were forcing her to go to some stupid movie premiere, which she totally didn't want to do. Her mother's stylist had shoved some annoying prissy dress on her and even stuck a bow in her hair plus swiped on lipstick—lipstick of all things!—and she felt like an idiot. Besides, she had two skinned knees, and everyone would know she wasn't a dress-up kind of girl anyhow, so what was the point?

These movie premieres were the worst—she felt like an animal at the zoo. Her parents put on their acting faces and slathered her with false affection for the cameras as they stood in front of the step and repeat banner—the one with the movie name repeated like wallpaper. There, they posed for photographers who took a million and one pictures of them and pretended to want to be there.

Zoey had been doing these things since she was a baby—her mother called them dog and pony shows. Although she felt more like Koko the Gorilla, with everyone pointing at them and popping off pictures like she was some freak exotic animal.

She never paid attention to whatever her parents were starring in. This was a business in her family and she was a kind of prop for them, to be honest. It was good business for them to appear to be kind, warm, loving parents, and as talented actors, they did a good job of pulling that off.

Her mother held her hand and her father wrapped his arm around her mother as they walked toward the banner. And that's when she caught a glimpse of him—Tanner, the kid she was with when she saw their parents naked. Standing with his gross parents. The boy she never ever wanted to see again because it made her want to throw up thinking about what they'd seen together. It was beyond embarrassing. How was she to know his parents were involved with this stupid movie?

The sound of the crowds gathering for the premiere grew louder in her ears. Or maybe it was her heart beating harder, pumping the blood through her veins too fast. The whole thing was awful. She couldn't look at his parents without seeing them stark naked, his dad with that, that, that *thing* sticking out like it did. His mother with some man's hands on her private parts like he was petting a dog.

Before she could pull herself away, her mother guided Zoey up to the banner right alongside Tanner's family, and damn if she wasn't stuck standing right next to him, which made it all the worse. Her face must be the color of that tomato sauce Mr. Puck always made for her when her parents dragged her to Spago's for dinner.

She tried to pretend Tanner wasn't there but then the photographers were telling them to hold hands and God, no, she couldn't touch him! His father's icky thing had been sticking out at the swimming pool. It was all so dreadful. Tanner was reaching for her hand—he told her he always followed the rules—and she kept trying to shake her hand away like she had a dead bug stuck to it she needed to get rid of, but the photographers were insisting.

"Zoey, grab the boy's hand," her mother said through gritted teeth with one of those fake smiles that said, "I'm going to spank you with a wooden spoon so hard your butt is going to be too sore to sit on if you don't listen to me," while telling the cameras she was the best mother on the planet.

Just as Tanner's fingers clasped around her hand, Zoey couldn't help herself. She drew back her right arm, as if she'd actually done this before, pivoted her body, putting the full force of herself into it, and *ka-pow*, her nine-year-old fist made contact with Tanner's nose. There was a loud gasp and her knuckles hurt and then he screamed out. Her mother grabbed her by the arm so hard she thought it might be dislocated at the shoulder.

And then Tanner was crying loud, aching sobs. He clutched on to his mother, and his nose was bleeding. Zoey was dragged away like a rag doll, but she could see him crying and bleeding and she felt bad, but she couldn't help herself, it was all so awful. And she kept hearing him cry.

When the movie reviews came out the next day her father was reading the paper over breakfast and looked up over the top edge of the paper while she pushed a soggy bite of pancake around in a puddle of syrup with her fork. It was a wonder she could sit at the table because her butt was so sore from the wooden spoon spanking she received.

"I don't know what you were thinking, young lady," her father said to her in that stern voice that dads used to scare children, "but that was unacceptable behavior." He then turned to look at her mother and winked. "That said, you did us all a bit of a favor. Because we knew this movie would bomb at the box office, but as they say, no such thing as bad publicity. You'll probably bring thousands more people to the theaters to see this stinker with that bizarre little maneuver of yours."

Her mother laughed, a tinkly little laugh that made her sound like the ingénue she wanted the world to think she was.

Zoey felt horrible for what she'd done to Tanner. But she had no way to even apologize to him. This would be the first of many lessons on why she wasn't cut out to be the daughter of movie stars.

Chapter Three

ANONYMITY was Tanner Eliasson's most prized possession. Which was saying a lot because he owned a stunning home on a sprawling ranch with a commanding view of the snowcapped peaks of the Rocky Mountains in northwest Montana. There, sunsets cast a fire of blazing orange along the mountain range so breathtaking, you'd want to cry. He was a stone's throw away from pristine lakes and hundreds of miles of spectacular hiking and biking trails that probed deep into the Montana wilderness. In the winter, he could be on the slopes in ten minutes. In the summer, he often took a brisk sail before breakfast and was back in the office in time for a full workday.

But being able to be him, not subservient to his less-than-charming past, well, he couldn't put a price tag on that. Tanner had made the decision long ago to sever ties with Tanner Cox, son of the famous film star Gina LeFevre and revered director Brady Cox. As soon as he was old enough to shake off the suffocating confines of his parents' fame and fortune, he took off, first for college, then vet school, and finally, here, to Montana, where he could be himself, no pretenses, no hiding from mockery, and no longer frozen out beneath the long shadow cast by his parents' larger-than-life world. And no Tanner Cox.

He'd gone so far as to drop his surname, instead substituting his middle name, Eliasson. He figured no one would put two and two together to link him with that part of his life that he had no interest in revisiting.

Tanner pulled up to the lake and parked the car. He dropped his kayak into the water and eased himself in. He savored being alone with his thoughts while out on the glassy early-morning lake. Usually it was a time for him to think about the medical history of some of his more perplexing veterinary cases. But today, for some reason he had his own history on his mind. It was like that for him: every so often Tanner couldn't help but reflect on his dark past, if only to take a deep breath and relish that he was living the opposite kind of existence now: no reporters, no paparazzi, no film studio machine to orchestrate his behavior within a thousand miles of here.

He'd certainly not enjoyed the trappings of fame. Not one bit. And things only got worse on that fateful night when that damned girl, Zoey Richards—he'd never forget her name—up and coldcocked him in front of the cameras at the premiere of his father's latest drama. Jesus, things went to shit fast after that happened. First off, it hurt like a son of a bitch. Who knew a nine-year-old could punch like that? He should've known—she was such a tomboy. But then, man, his face throbbed, his nose was gushing like a damned fire hydrant, and he'd soon learn it was broken.

At the time, he did the first thing you do when something unexpectedly awful happens to you—you seek comfort from someone you hope will actually go to the trouble of comforting you. But he was sad to realize that someone—his mother—was more upset his blood was ruining the designer gown she'd chosen for this special evening than she was about his welfare. Pretty quickly, a cadre of studio lackeys swarmed them all, mostly to try to salvage her gown, but one underling had the presence of mind to stick some cocktail napkins underneath his nostrils to staunch the blood flow. Crying like a girl in front of all those cameras had been an embarrassment, but he learned quickly that his father was even more mortified than he was.

"Stop crying, or I'll give you something to cry about," he'd hissed into Tanner's ear. Tanner sobbed a little longer and stopped except for a few gasping sighs here and there.

That was the day that Tanner decided he would man up, the way his father had so wanted him to. No more tears, no more emotion, no more nothing. Shame it was too late—the next morning the tabloids had given him his own unwanted moniker: the Weeping Wimp. The *Variety* headline read "Teary Tanner." Nowhere did Zoey get called out for decking him for no good reason. Instead Tanner carried the shame for having done nothing but show up at his father's stupid film premiere and get punched in the face, and it would take him years to live down the lingering embarrassment from that night.

All the kids at school teased him mercilessly. He was ostracized even more than he had been before for simply being a bit of a loner. Girls giggled at him; boys mocked him. Were it not for Sunshine, his life would have been a perpetual state of hell. She's the thing that helped him get through it. God, he missed that girl to this day. She'd passed away when he was still in college, but it seemed like only yesterday. The first thing he did when he opened his practice out here in Montana was get another Lab pup. Suki was a four-month-old snowball of a pup, white as a polar bear with the most adorable edge of toasted marshmallow to her ears. Suki was his family now, albeit a mischievous one.

It had been years since he'd been back to Hollywood. His parents were older now. Last year his father came out of semiretirement to shoot a film he'd hoped would be his great comeback. It flopped. Tanner felt sort of sorry for him, but he also didn't see the need to swoop in and soothe the man's bruised ego. What goes around comes around in the world.

His mother occasionally did guest-starring roles on sitcoms playing the latest ingénue's mother. He could only imagine how mortifying that was for her, her countenance puffy from age-denying injections, her unlined forehead resembling an overly starched sheet on a military-style bed. She could never smile due to all that Botox, which was a bit ironic, considering how she'd mastered the fake smile as a starlet. Now it was a look that was denied her merely due to her refusing to look her age. Vanity, thy name was still Gina LeFevre.

Sometimes he felt guilty about not being a doting son. But it was hard to gin up love and affection for two people who might have given him life but certainly didn't give him joie de vivre. Attention from his folks had been sparse, so the role reversal seemed a natural progression. He made a mental note to maybe give them a call sometime to see how they were doing, but he'd likely forget.

He'd been kayaking for more than an hour, taking note of an eagle soaring overhead. Nearby a heron alighted from a rush. Along the shore, a beaver was hard at work damming in a quiet cove. It had taken Tanner long enough to get out to Montana, but he'd known the minute he settled here that this was home for him. All those years wishing he'd had a home, and it had been waiting for him, right here, all along, none of that baggage from his past life to cause him troubles, thank goodness.

Chapter Four

IF there was one thing worse than Zoey Richards' parents telling her what to do, it was when she chose to ignore them and they were proven right. Damned if that didn't piss her off. And in this case, it was doubly bad because while they were right, it meant her entire life's course had now taken an about-face, and certainly not in the direction she'd intended it to go.

It all started when she met a handsome man named Rodrigo when she'd been on holiday in the Dominican Republic. Tall, muscular, with wavy brown hair and provocative brown eyes, he was her skydiving instructor. When he was spooning her from midair for the plunge at eight thousand feet from the airplane, it was impossible not to feel as one with the man.

Following a few postjump celebratory glasses of champagne, she'd been lubricated enough to think it was a great idea to have sex with him. And, well, he was pretty darned good in bed, not to mention hung like a horse. What was a girl to do when he cooed all those sweet words in Spanish? *Muy caliente mi amor*, indeed.

It wasn't like Zoey to sleep with a guy so readily, but considering he'd practically held her life in his hands, it seemed as if they'd been together for much longer than a few short hours. Besides, didn't everyone bond over life-and-death circumstances?

She and Rodrigo hit it off in a big way, and by the end of the week she was convinced he was the man for her, and he seemed more than willing to uproot himself and move to LA to prove it to her.

Her outwardly prim-and-proper mother (although, come off it, Zoey knew that was all a ruse; she'd seen her at that pool party with that boy Tanner's father and suffice it to say, she was not a blushing virgin) was aghast that she'd hooked up with Rodrigo, not to mention that she brought him home and moved him into the guest cottage she was temporarily using on her parents' sprawling Malibu property. Yeah, she hated that she'd been sponging off her super annoying parents, but she'd recently quit her job selling real estate, sold her condo in Santa Monica, and was trying to figure out what to do next when she'd taken that little vacay in the Caribbean. With Rodrigo coming back with her, she'd conveniently been spinning her wheels—while having pretty great sex—ever since.

A free place to crash for a while was the least her parents could do after forcing her to be an only child under their tutelage during her formative years. If their pattern of selfish behavior hadn't scarred her, nothing could've. Except, maybe Rodrigo, who seemed to be the last straw.

It turned out he was decidedly not a one-woman man. In fact, based on a series of group text messages that Zoey stumbled upon on his phone, he was instead a many-woman man. All at the same time. With pictures to prove it. And had evidently been sleeping his way through the Greater Los Angeles Swappers Club for the past six months until Zoey intercepted his texts and put an end to it. He was probably still swapping away, but she did put an end to his free ride in Malibu and ix-nayed the pending nuptials a mere two days before the big day as soon as she read him the riot act and

18

threw in a few Spanish invectives she'd learned along the way. After she shoved his belongings into a large black garbage bag, she hurled them out the door then off a nearby cliff into the raging Pacific Ocean below.

If Zoey were honest with herself, she'd admit she hadn't truly been in love with Rodrigo. But she had been in lust with him, so she was sad to say farewell to the impassioned Latin lover thing she'd gotten quite used to. Aside from that, it was the sting of knowing her mother was right that resonated with her even weeks after she'd learned of his betrayal.

She'd gone up to her parent's house because the wedding cake—one of the few things she'd forgotten to cancel—had been delivered and her mother no doubt wanted to rub her face in it a bit.

"Did I not tell you he was going to hurt you?" Her mother took a large sip of her third old-fashioned (before three in the afternoon, natch) as she berated Zoey in the sunny, brightly lit, all-white kitchen in her parents' house. On the countertop nearby, sat the offending wedding cake, mocking poor Zoey. "But did you listen to me? Of course not. God forbid your mother is ever right about anything."

Zoey often hated to look at her mother; she had such a dour smirk that seemed permanently secured to her visage. For a woman who plastered on a fake smile throughout her acting career, it sure hadn't seemed to stick. Zoey couldn't help but stare at her mother's mouth, the pouty kisser that was once plastered on a billboard in Times Square, back when she had a fat contract with a makeup line. Was it Maybelline or Cover Girl? She noticed her coral lipstick seeping into the fissures that led from her mother's lips like tiny tributaries leading to a mighty river. A thicket of spittle adhered itself to the corner of her mouth. How the mighty had fallen. *Wow. When did my mother become as ugly on the outside as she's long been on the inside?*

For ten minutes her mother chastised her without response.

"I told your father you weren't blessed with either my good sense or my looks, for that matter. Is that why you do these things? Because you're not as pretty as I am?"

Zoey squinted. What the hell was wrong with this woman? Zoey would rather have looked like two-day-old roadkill than look like her mother if it meant sharing her narcissistic personality. Because everything seemed to come down to Alexa Lipari and nothing else.

Sticking her finger out, she swiped between layers of her blueberry lemon curd deconstructed wedding cake, trying to ignore her mother's drunken rant. As she licked the curd off her finger, a blueberry dropped onto her silk shirt. Dammit, she couldn't even enjoy her failed wedding cake without suffering further indignities.

"And what's the deal with this wedding cake?" Her mother waggled a wobbly pointer finger toward the somewhat barren-looking cake. It sat by its lonesome near the six-burner Wolf cooktop her mother never used because, determined to remain a size zero until she died, she never cooked and never ate.

Zoey had half a mind to shove that cake right up Alexa's ass, but she'd never be able to get it around her Spanx.

"What do you mean what's the deal?" Zoey said. "There's no wedding."

"Leave it to you to have a naked wedding cake," her mother said. "Considering how you couldn't keep your clothes on with that man long enough to learn that he was as bad as we said he was."

Zoey held up her hands. She'd had enough. "Okay, Mom, cut it out. I know you think you've won now that I'm not getting married. And I don't understand why you would see that as a victory. But okay, whatever. At least I'm not a sexual deviant like you are."

Her mother's face went red with rage and she stood up. "How dare you speak to me that way," she said, throwing back her old-fashioned in one long gulp. "At least I would have enough class to not have a naked wedding cake."

Zoey had hit her limit. She was over this woman. She stood up, walked to the cake, and slid her fingers beneath it, palms up, securing a solid grip on it. She took two steps toward where Alexa sat perched, cross-legged, swilling a bourbon drink, and launched it, smack into her face, leaving her dripping with lemon curd. Never had her mother's face looked so appealing. Zoey dusted off her hands, licking some of the lemon curd from her fingers, then turned and walked out of the kitchen, out the front door, and out of her parents' lives for good.

Simply because her mother might have been right didn't mean she had to be right in a my-way-or-the-highway kinda way. A normal mother would have comforted her in her sadness. But that wasn't in her mother's wheelhouse. Maybe this was what Zoey needed to finally grab life by the horns and ride it. She returned to the cottage, called a moving company to come pack up her belongings, filled two suitcases with life's necessities, rounded up her Persian kitty, Snowball and all of her accoutrements, loaded up her Mercedes sedan, and pulled away from her Pacific Coast Highway lair, bound for the great unknown.

Chapter Five

IT hadn't taken Zoey long to decide where she was going to go. Her best friend Izzy had a beautiful cabin in Banff that she'd offered Zoey to use at any time. She knew she'd be okay with her using it but called once she got past Vegas to make sure.

"What the hell is going on Zo?"

Zoey laid on her horn as some Mercedes sports coup cut her off on the highway.

"What is going on is Zoey is hitting the road," she said.

"As in going somewhere for the weekend?"

"As in checking out of LA for a while and getting far away from my monstrous mother. I thought maybe it would be perfect to head up to your cabin for a little while to lick my wounds."

Izzy sighed. "Oh, sweetie. I'm sorry you're in this position. I know you wished things had worked out with Rodrigo, but I'm glad you aren't going ahead with it."

Zoey shook her head. "Don't tell me you didn't trust him either." She put her blinker on and got in the left lane to pass a tractor trailer.

"Oh gosh, no. I'm glad because I didn't lose my girlfriend to holy matrimony." She laughed. "I know that sounds selfish, but so I'm selfish. I was dreading losing my partner in crime."

"Yeah, well, you might be losing her anyhow. I'm

heading inland for a while."

"That sounds like a crazy notion. And leave the beach behind?"

Zoey shrugged. "I know. I love the ocean. I really do. And I love you too. But it feels like the right time for a new start, you know?"

"So you packed it all up?"

"Yeah, pretty much. I called the movers to box everything else up, but I have the essentials. Plus Snowball."

"Awww, Snowy-wowwy has to go with?" she said in baby talk.

"Sorry, I know you love my little white furball, but she's my spirit animal. I have to bring her along."

"I've never heard of Persian cats as spirit animals. Isn't it supposed to be some sort of wild thang?"

"You ever get scratched by her claws? You might reconsider thinking she's a tame kitty cat."

"I know Snowball wouldn't hurt a flea."

"So you're good with Snow and me heading to your place?"

"Absolutely. Though I might head up there in two weeks with that hot guy from HR I went on a date with last week."

"Um, three's a crowd, though, no?"

"Oh, it'll be okay."

"You're so lying to me. No doubt it's an itty bitty cabin. I would hear you two having hot monkey sex all night long." Zoey flicked her phone to hands-free. "Worse yet, Snowball would start making those caterwauling sounds. She'd think some tomcat was after her. It'd freak her out."

"Let's cross that bridge when we get there," her friend said. "In the meantime, don't drink the milk in the fridge. It's like eight months old."

"Yuk."

"Don't eat anything in the fridge for that matter. You'd have to get your stomach pumped."

"In other words, you didn't clean when you left last time."

"Don't act so surprised."

"Of course not. You don't clean the apartment you live in—why would you clean that?" Zoey smiled. "No worries. I've got your back, and I'll have it so clean you'll eat off the floor in no time."

"I want you to take it easy and get past this heartache."

"To be honest, Izzy, I'm more burned up about my folks than I am about Rodrigo. I'm sick of them."

"Yeah, well, your mother has always been pretty unkind toward you."

"Right?" Zoey took a deep breath. "But you know I'm not one to waste time dwelling on the past."

"Like when that girl Suzy Leoni pulled your skirt down at school that one day and everyone saw your underwear?"

"Ugh, don't remind me. But yeah. I mean what was the point of moaning about it? I moved on, got a little even with her—"

"When you traded her brownies for ones with a laxative in them."

Zoey laughed. "That was the best revenge, wasn't it?"

"Award-winning."

"But seriously. As far as I'm concerned, the past is long since over and I'm all about the future. In fact, I want nothing to do with anyone whatsoever from my past."

"Uh, except me?"

Zoey nodded. "Of course. Except you. From here on out, I'm starting from scratch. Destination: Banff, Alberta, Canada."

Zoey was well into day two of her drive when she exited off the highway near some dinky-looking boomtown called Bristol, Montana, to fill up the tank. She'd felt horrible keeping Snowball trapped in her kitty carrier, as she'd been keeping up a mournful meow for what seemed like hours. So, at last, about an hour ago she'd let her out of the cage to wander in the back seat of the car.

Zoey filled up her car, then decided to follow the signs to a nearby coffee shop, hoping to get a cappuccino for the road. The light was changing as she approached Main Street, so she came to a full stop rather than trying to get through before it turned red. Unfortunately the idiot driver behind her didn't have the same plan, and instead rammed smack into the back of her SUV, not hard enough to deploy the air bags, but certainly with enough impact to send Snowball flying into the front seat, letting out a piercing wail.

Zoey threw her car in park and carefully grabbed her frightened cat, pulling her toward her chest, stroking her head and trying to elicit a purr, which would indicate some level of contentment. The driver of the vehicle that hit her got out of her car and rushed to the driver's side window.

"I'm so sorry," she said. "I didn't mean to do that. I picked my kids up at school and we were going for ice cream and the baby started crying and I turned to see what was wrong and then this." She spread her arms out in despair.

Zoey held up her hands. She could tell the poor woman was frazzled. "It's okay. Accidents happen. Literally." She looked back to see how badly her trunk had been crunched. She didn't want to leave her kitty in the car while she went to look. "But I do want to find a vet to check Snowball out. She went flying through the car. So maybe can we exchange information, then do you know where the nearest veterinarian's office might be?"

The woman nodded as she yelled back to her kids she'd be right there. "I'm so sorry. Truly I am. Here's my info," she handed Zoey a card. "You can take a picture of it and get all my insurance details from that. And then maybe I'll go around you, and you can follow me to Dr. Eliasson's office? It's just a couple of blocks away." She extended her hand. "I'm Amy, by the way. Amy Wardman. And I'm truly sorry."

"Look, we'll figure this out. Let me get Snowball looked at. Hopefully the trunk is fine and we'll be on our way."

The woman scrunched her nose, which Zoey pretended not to notice. The last thing she wanted was to get stuck in this little one-horse town in the middle of Godforsaken, Montana. She'd do her best to be out of there in an hour, tops.

Chapter Six

TANNER was beat. He'd been up kayaking at dawn, had surgeries all morning long, followed by a five-mile run at lunchtime. Then he'd taken Suki on a walk because she was too young to run distances yet. And so far, the afternoon had been one emergency after another, from a bunny that had a cough that wouldn't stop to a pregnant Saint Bernard who kept throwing up.

He glanced at his watch: forty minutes till he could close up and get out of here, providing no more crises for the day. It was one of those days where you knew summer was here to stay for a while, and he was anxious to hit the rooftop bar at Harry's, where he could enjoy the view of the Rockies while sipping on a nice, cold IPA, listening to his friend Sully play acoustic guitar, and letting all the pretty girls oooh and ahhh over his puppy while he enjoyed the view of them bent over, their cleavages on display as they petted his pup. It was a win-win for all.

That might have sounded crass, but he didn't mean it to be. He didn't want to get caught in a relationship with anyone, so it was far easier to relish the scenery from afar. Plus with tourist season underway, most of the women he'd meet at a bar around here would be out-of-towners, and he sure didn't want to get himself into some long-distance relationship that would go nowhere fast.

Cindy Hardison, one of his vet techs, entered the exam

room as he was washing his hands.

"Dr. Eliasson, you have two more patients scheduled, but I think Dr. Cuoco can take them. I've got an emergency that came in and I thought you'd be best with it."

She handed him a chart with some information on it.

"Cat's name is Snowball," he said under his breath, scanning his finger across the notes the tech had handed him. "A two-year-old Persian in a fender bender." He shrugged. "Fine. Go ahead and send them in." He scrubbed his hands over his face. Maybe he'd head home after this and chill out in the hot tub instead.

"Dr. Eliasson, this is Zoey Richards."

Tanner, who'd been busy spraying disinfectant on the exam table, glanced up when he heard the name. Zoey Richards. Impossible. There must be plenty of women named Zoey Richards out there. No way could it be her.

But the woman turned the corner into the room and he'd have to have been deaf, dumb, and blind not to know who she was. The dead giveaway was her eyes: way back when, it seemed they took up half her face. But she'd grown into them. They were still large, but attractively so, with that sort of damp, liquid, endangered baby seal look to them that made you think she'd been crying and needed a hug. Well, a hug sure as hell wasn't on the agenda. Then he saw her dimples—her broad smile put them on display, making her damned face light up like the night sky.

She was no longer the scrawny tomboy, that's for sure. She was in shape, but shapely, with a perfect little waistline and tits that filled out her red tee—the one that said "Demon Seed" on it, go figure—perfectly. Then there were those runner's legs, long and lean and strong. He made a mental note to check out her ass as soon as he could do so discreetly. Not that it mattered.

He was going to find out what the hell she was doing in his exam room and promptly pawn her off on Dr. Cuoco, and he'd take whatever else came his way today, even if it was a surly crocodile with a toothache. He realized the only slight nod to her former tomboy self might have been her brown highlighted hair. Sure, back then it was long and straight, but now it had a sort of boyish cut to it, short and gold-streaked and layered but kind of sexy, like Charlize Theron's hair. In another universe, were it not the girl who'd ruined his childhood, he wouldn't have thought twice about entertaining how amazing it would be to strip her naked and learn every inch of that rockin' body of hers, but no way. Not with Zoey "Slugger" Richards.

Damn, for someone who ruined his life all those years ago, she sure did grow into a beautiful woman.

He shook his head to clear the memories and extended a hand. He was going to presume she didn't know who he was, which would make it all the easier to ditch her in a few minutes. She'd never know the difference, and Calvin Cuoco would take great care of her cat.

"Nice to meet you Mrs.—" not that he was wondering, but, yeah, maybe he was wondering.

She frowned. "Well, if that's not complicated, nothing is."

He knit his brows. "Oh?"

She looked up at a calendar on the wall, one of those with cute kittens in different poses for each month. She pointed at the little squares on the calendar and counted to herself.

"Well, I'll be," she said. "If it weren't for that little ratfink Rodrigo, I would, in fact, be a Mrs. in three days' time." She pressed her cat to her chest more tightly.

Tanner squinted at her, not knowing what the fuck she

was talking about and having no intention of seeking clarification. "All righty then, not that that's any of my business. So, who's this we have here?"

She shook her head. "Oh God, did I actually say those things? I'm so sorry. That was super weird. Um." She bit her lip. "Look, I was stopped at an intersection. The woman behind me kept going, whacked into my car a bit. Snowball went flying into the front seat."

"The cat wasn't secured in a cat carrier?"

"Well, she was, but then she wasn't."

"Did it break or something?"

She waved her hand. "It's a long story. But I left LA like two days ago and, I mean, she's a cat. They hate being in those things, even to go to the vet—nothing personal. But to be in jail like that all day long for days, well, you can imagine how upset she was."

Well, no kidding, he thought. No animal likes to be locked in a cage, but sometimes it's for its own good.

"So was she in a cage or not?"

"She kept meowing. Over and over. She sounded like a dump truck had run over her ovaries, it was that mournful."

Tanner suppressed a smile. She was a bit of a smart-ass. He liked that in a woman. Except he was never going to like that in this woman. Because he was never going to deal with this woman again. She was persona non grata in his life.

"Not precisely sure what that sound would be, but I'll take your word for it."

He nodded to his assistant Cindy to hand him the cat, who shrieked and took a hard swipe at his arm, drawing four even slices down his forearm.

"Oh, shit," his old nemesis said. "Shit, shit, shit, shit, shit. I'm so sorry." She rifled through her purse and pulled out a wadded up tissue with which she quickly began to dab the blood that was trickling from his wounds. God only knew what germs were on that tissue, but it sure didn't look like it was particularly sterile. She probably used it to blow her nose before she'd pressed it to his flesh. Tanner held up his hand.

"That's quite all right," he said. My vet tech can get me some antibiotic cream and I'll be fine. Happens all the time."

He didn't want to tell her this was the first cat to scratch him in two years. Figures it'd be her cat to break the streak.

"Let's get down to business here," he said as Cindy helped hold the cat so she'd not draw any more blood. He took down Snowball's vital signs, checked out her overall body condition, and examined her eyes, ears, nose, mouth, and teeth. He checked to see if there was bruising beneath that heavy coat of fur, then listened to her breathing and measured her pulse.

"Okay, let's see how she's moving," he said, assessing the symmetry of the musculature and the cat's mobility. Then he palpated her abdomen to feel her organs, then her lymph nodes, and eventually tested her neurologic responses.

"By all outward appearances Snowball seems to have fared fine," he said. "Although I wouldn't mind keeping her overnight for observation to be sure."

Zoey pursed her lips.

"Something wrong with that?"

She shook her head. "It's only that I'm headed up to Banff and I've got a lot more driving to do."

He held up his hands. "I'm not going to make you do it. But I think it's not a bad idea to be sure there's nothing happening internally. Especially if you're traveling with a cat, they get stressed out easily without adding a car accident into the mix. Cats like their routines."

Zoey frowned. "You sure that's necessary? I mean maybe I can get back in the car and go find a vet in Banff tomorrow?"

Tanner looked at his watch. "At this rate, you'll not get there till late. What if there's something wrong with Snowball? You're not going to have anyone to help you out at that point. I'm not going to tell you what to do, but I'll tell you what I'd do if I were you, and that would be to leave her here overnight. I'm sure you can find a hotel in town and get on the road by morning."

The last thing he wanted was to have her remain in his little town for any longer than possible. But he also couldn't shirk his responsibilities as a vet to ensure that her cat was treated to the best of his abilities.

She sighed. "Fine," she said as she buried her nose into the top of Snowball's head. "But you all better take good care of my kitty. She's all I've got now."

Tanner gave her a nod. "Smart decision. I'll pass you off to Cindy, here, who can get Snowball all set up."

He slipped out of the exam room as fast as possible, wanting to put as much distance as he could between him and the Muhammad Ali of Rodeo Drive. He'd let Dr. Cuoco speak with her in the morning and he'd be completely done with Zoey Richards once and for all.

Chapter Seven

ZOEY figured since she was stuck here overnight, it wouldn't hurt to have her car checked out to be sure there weren't any lingering problems from the accident.

Garth Newell, the mechanic at some shop down the road from the veterinary office, kept the shop open an extra hour for her while he inspected her Mercedes. To her great dismay, he had bad news.

"Just as I suspected—not even thinking about the body work you're gonna need on this thing, right now you've got to deal with transmission damage. Looks like it'll be at least two days till I get the parts in that I need to fix it."

"Two days?"

"Could even be longer with the weekend coming up."

"What if I take my chances and get it fixed when I get to Banff?"

He shrugged, holding his greasy hands palms up. "Ma'am, you can do what you want. But you start having slipping problems with your transmission, and you're going to regret not getting that thing fixed."

She scowled at him. "Well is it dangerous?"

He laughed. "Sure, it can be dangerous. You might start having internal parts rattling around in there, which messes up your shifting, and the transmission could get stuck in a gear or shift into the wrong gear. You run the risk of broken pieces of metal falling into your coolant and being forced through the cooling system, which is going to give you a whole load of more grief than you already have right now."

This day was devolving rapidly and Zoey wasn't happy about it. All she wanted was to get up to Banff and settle in and relax, have a couple of glasses of wine while soaking in the hot tub, and have some long-needed sleep. The last thing she wanted was to be trapped in this cow town.

"So," she said, tracing her toe along a large splotch of oil on the garage floor. "You're telling me you'd wait it out for the repair?"

He nodded. "You betcha."

Well, crap. Here she was, stuck in this darned town, with both her cat and her car in jail. What the heck was she going to do now?

She reached into the back seat for her overnight bag. She was gonna have to trust that the rest of her stuff would be safe with the mechanic. In the meantime, she was going to roll her wheeled suitcase down Main Street until she could find a spot to pull over to make some calls in search of a hotel room.

After walking about a block and a half, she found a coffee shop, which seemed as good a place as any to do a hotel search. She opened the door and the bell attached to the hinge chimed as she entered. It was like a coffee shop she'd expect to find in the land of ranches and cowboys and wide-open spaces. A smattering of stuffed animal heads mounted on the warm, cedar walls, with a massive bison and a few of those sheep with the massive horns that get into big fights on cliffs peered down at her. It was a coffee shop-slash-gift shop, and they had cute little knickknacks of local flavor: dish towels, cattle horn (because what self-respecting mantel would be without one?), stuffed bears, and buffalo and the like. It was a cute shop, and in one corner, a fire blazed, even in mid-June. But then again that was very LA of them—everyone she knew had a fire going in their house despite how hot it was outside. It made for a cozier scene.

As she approached the gleaming pine counter, a woman who looked to be about thirty-five, her skin tanned, her smile white, her hair in two long braids, came out from a back room.

"Oh, hey," she said, pursing her lips. "I hate to tell you, but we're closed for the evening."

Zoey looked around and realized there weren't any other patrons in the place.

"Sorry, I meant to lock the front door but hadn't gotten to it yet."

Zoey knit her brows. "Well, is there someplace you'd recommend I could go to get on my phone and find a hotel?"

The woman thrust her lip out in a pout. "It seems I'm the bearer of bad news tonight." She leaned over the counter, handing her a copy of a small local paper. "The Western Governors' Conference starts here tomorrow. I'd be surprised if you could find a place to stay right now."

"You've got to be kidding me." Zoey rolled her eyes. Of course it figured. She was in the middle of nowhere and couldn't find a place to rest her head. Not even in her car!

"It's Wednesday night," the lady said. "They have music on the rooftop at Harry's. It's a fabulous view, really nice folk, and they've got Wi-Fi. Why don't you head up there for a while, relax, and get on your phone and try to find some places maybe outside of town a bit."

"I don't even have a way to get out of town. Do you have Uber around here?"

She laughed. "We have Uber ish."

"Uber ish?"

"Yeah well, there's Uber when someone decides they

need some money and they're gonna drive. If it's your lucky night, you've got yourself a ride."

Zoey refrained from muttering curses because it wasn't this woman's fault. No sense in shooting the messenger.

"I do have one other idea that might work. There's an outdoor store about a block away from here. They're open till eleven. They have a tent display in the back of the store. I bet if you're really quiet, you could park yourself inside one of those tents and no one would even know you were there."

Zoey burst out laughing, then squinted at her. "You're serious, aren't you?"

The woman nodded and held out her hand. "Sorry, should've introduced myself. I'm Susy Russell. Hate to be such a bearer of bad news, but I hope my advice can help you a little in a bind."

Zoey struggled to imagine in what world would she sleep illegally in a tent in a retail store. Shit. Well, she was going to get on the phone and keep calling till she found something. Surely there would be something, somewhere, that would have a bed and bathroom for her for the night.

After taking the wrong turn out of the coffee shop and ending up in the parking lot of a grocery store, she entered the name of the bar into the GPS on her phone and followed the path for the next two blocks till she happened upon it. The only good news about this town was it was so small you'd never get lost. When she got to the bar, there was a line with a good twenty people in front of her. *Figures, the whole town goes to the only bar in town, duh.* The hostess told her it would be a forty-minute wait, which helped to cement Zoey's sour mood. With no place to sit, she parked her butt on the curb in front, near a few squalling children who'd gotten into a race and ended up with skinned knees.

She pulled up her favorite travel app and started

searching for hotel rooms. At first she was excited—there were some nice-looking hotels in the area. It turned out the town was the base to a ski resort as well as close enough to Glacier National Park, and the town attracted gobs of tourists, plus a lot of outdoors enthusiasts. Which meant it was even less likely she'd find someplace to rest her weary head. God forbid she have a fender bender in a normal damned town.

But her enthusiasm melted into a puddle of doom and gloom at her feet as she discovered that everything was indeed booked. Next she opened her Airbnb app, assuming surely somewhere there would be a bed available. Her face fell when she learned the only available place remaining within a hundred miles was a teepee—seriously, a damned teepee—that someone built for fun in some remote woods. Which would mean she'd be alone in the woods with probably a couple of psychopaths looking to murder lonely women, and also she'd have to pee in the woods and would get poison ivy or a rattlesnake bite on her ass. Or maybe a bear would carry her off to her lair where she would feed her, piece by piece, to her babies.

She was greatly relieved when the hostess called her name and she was offered entrée into the coveted sanctuary of Harry's rooftop bar. After climbing four flights of steps—and gasping for air by the second flight—she arrived at the rooftop bar, which was indeed crowded. She scoured the scene, trying to figure out where to go. She didn't want to stand because, well, first off, she had her damned suitcase with her and that would be particularly weird, and secondly, a woman standing alone at a bar with a suitcase smacked of desperation. She noticed the one end of the bar had people clustered together chatting and laughing. The other end featured a guy seated on a stool with one of those mics on those extender arms in front of him, strumming a guitar while wailing about some girl who done him wrong or something like that. Zoey needed a drink because some guy had sure as hell done her wrong. So, she figured the patrons down at this end of the bar were her people.

As luck would have it, there was one seat open, which faced the beautiful tableau of Rocky Mountains with the waning sun, washing the sky with its apricot light. Okay, so this wasn't so bad. Pretty view. Weird to have your back to the entertainment but also made it easier to avoid small talk with strangers, which was fine by her. Last time she made small talk with a stranger, she brought him home to LA and got engaged to him. Everyone knew how that one worked out. No command performances, thanks.

Zoey tucked her suitcase in close to her feet beneath the long countertop where she sat. She didn't want to be completely rude and turned herself partially so it wouldn't appear she was ignoring the entertainment. The guy with the guitar was good-looking, with scruffy caramel hair, maybe a little in need of a haircut. His green eyes were the color of some semiprecious stone that was probably once mined near here. He had that air about him that he was imminently likable, the kind of guy you'd confide in and complain to about your boyfriend.

She shook her head. She clearly had been alone for too long, considering she was creating an entire life around a strange dude with a guitar. The waitress came by and took her order. Zoey was ready for a fat burger and a cold beer. One nice thing about being away from LA was not having to worry about people judging you for what you put in your mouth. If she were back there, she'd have ordered the microgreens with chia seeds and would probably go home and eat Ben and Jerry's out of the carton while standing by the kitchen sink. It was good not having anyone around who cared about you. Well, good and bad.

"That's my seat, you know." Zoey glanced over her shoulder to see a grizzled-looking thirty-something guy with spittle-coated lips pointing at her.

"I'm sorry, what did you say?" She frowned at him, hoping to send him the "get the hell out of here" juju so he'd leave her alone.

"I got up to take a dump and I come back and you're in my seat," the guy said, his words carrying the distinctive slur of someone on his umpteenth drink. She decided the best reaction was no reaction, so instead, she pulled out her phone and opened up Instagram.

As she scrolled down, Drunky McDrunkster kept hammering away at her.

"You think because of who you are you can do this to me, you're wrong," he said.

Which made her wonder who she was. Not like anyone on the planet would know her as anyone but Zoey Richards. She'd made it her job, all those years ago, to fly wayyy under the radar after that time when she slugged that kid at that movie premiere. She thought it would be one and done, but no, the press latched onto that forever, calling her all sorts of nicknames, like Muhammad Ali of Rodeo Drive, which was stupid because they were nowhere near Rodeo Drive. Someone pegged her Sugar Ray Slammer, and for a long time, even kids at school called her Slammer. It was all very humiliating because it was an accident and then that kid, whatever his name was, ugh, he blubbered on and on and wouldn't accept her apology and her parents barely spoke to her for a week afterward.

After that, her mother made her stop with the tomboy stuff—her stylist showed up one day with the most prissy outfits that her mother made her wear. All Zoey wanted to do was be herself and not have to deal with all the awfulness that came with her parents being famous movie stars. Next, it was bows in her hair and those horrid patent leather shoes and velvet and satin and it was sheer torture.

"Hey, lady. Hey, lady." She felt someone poking her in the side of her ribs. The drunk guy.

The waitress brought Zoey's burger and beer and Zoey gave her a "help me" glance, but the waitress shrugged and told Zoey the guy was harmless. Sure, harmless until the spit splattering her from his one-sided conversation ended up in her burger. Maybe she'd get some communicable disease from him and waste away and die before she got a chance to stop at the adorable pie shop she'd passed on her way to Harry's. Because, well, pie.

Wrapping her mouth wrapped around her burger, ready to dig in for a big bite, she felt the strange man's hands on her shoulders. Hands she was certain didn't get washed in the restroom when he'd gone in there, despite the signs posted in every restaurant bathroom in America urging patrons and employees alike to maintain a modicum of sanitary practices. Was that so much to ask for?

The man was pulling at her and he'd raised his voice even more, insisting she give him back his seat. She wanted to eat her burger in peace, darn it!

Then she felt him trying to physically lift her up and she'd had enough. She turned her body and reflexively drew back her arm, in a move that offered muscle memory from many years of boxing at the gym. She had a mean cross. Well, the whole world once knew that: the first time she ever hit anything was that dumb kid whose parents' house she'd been dragged to. But it wasn't till she grew up that she got into boxing for fun and exercise. It made her feel strong, which she loved.

"Hey, lady," the guy slurred even louder as he grabbed at her yet again, just as she'd positioned herself, poised to cross her left arm straight across to nail him.

Chapter Eight

TANNER felt the dark cloud lift the minute he got out of the exam room, thankful that he'd dodged that bullet. Make that mortar fire. Ding, dong, the witch was dead; he'd gotten rid of the slugger chick. She'd never be the wiser about his identity and she'd be gone by morning. *Adios, chica.*

After the last patient had gone, he took Suki outside to do her business, sat down to sift through some paperwork on his desk, then checked in on a few of his patients who were staying overnight. He had a vet tech on duty to keep an eye on animals that were boarding for the night, so he knew they were in good hands. After giving Snowball the once-over one more time, he grabbed his laptop bag and left the clinic, locking the door behind him.

He was torn about what to do. He'd promised Sully he'd come hear him play, but damn, he was tired. A promise was a promise though. If he were playing somewhere, he'd want his friends to support him. He definitely wasn't going home to change. He'd never make it out again if he did. Instead he gave a quick whistle to Suki, who came running toward him and hopped onto the passenger seat of his truck, where he seat belted her to her harness for the short drive. He drove the three blocks to Harry's, found a space not too far away, and entered through the back door. As any good local worth their salt knew, you never, ever, ever entered through the front door, where there'd be a line halfway around the block.

The front entrance was for newbies and tourists.

He gave a wave to the hostess, who scruffed Suki on the head, then he climbed the stairs two by two up to the rooftop terrace. He wouldn't stay long—only long enough to grab a quick dinner, have a beer or two, listen to a set, and get back home. Maybe then he'd have enough time to relax in the hot tub.

When Tanner got to the top, he grimaced at the crowd. He was so not into dealing with a mob of people. Give him the solace of a hike where all you hear is the wind whispering through the trees, and he was a happy man. Waving at a few folks he knew, he noticed someone getting up from a cushioned seat not far from the makeshift stage. This would be perfect—Suki could curl up in his lap and they could snuggle and relax for a while. As he grabbed the chair, he gave Sully a nod of acknowledgment. Sully was a little more bohemian than Tanner, what with his scruffy hair, bare feet, faded T-shirt, and threadbare jeans. Even after being at work all day, Tanner made sure he looked presentable. Not that you'd find him in a business suit, mind you; he lived in the Wild West, so his "business suit" was a pair of Patagonia pants and a Mountain Hardwear shirt that would be as useful rock climbing as it would be canoeing and dry in minutes.

The waitress came by to take his order, bending down to pet Suki. Tanner was friends with the waitstaff here, so it was not like he'd deliberately ogle any of these ladies, but it was hard not to, with their tight, scoop-neck T-shirts. It only served to remind him how long it had been since he'd been with a woman. Too damned long, even though he'd done this to himself. His last breakup hit him a little hard. It was with a woman he'd thought he could marry. But when she broke up with him because she didn't want to compete for his attention with, as she said verbatim, "a bunch of strangers' pets for the rest of her life," he was left questioning his good judgment. How could he, a vet, have ever chosen someone like that?

It was enough to give a man a crisis of confidence. The waitress delivered his beer and he took a big swig as Sully returned from a brief break. Usually it took the crowd a few minutes to settle into the music after the performers had walked away, but this time it was kind of annoying. Some guy nearby was loud and drunk and harassing a woman who was seated next to where he'd been standing. He wished the woman would take her damned boyfriend home so the rest of the customers wouldn't have to listen to it.

But even when Sully started strumming hard on the guitar, the voices of those two were rising higher and higher, eclipsing the music. Tanner was ticked off. He came here to relax, not to listen to some damned lover's quarrel.

"Hey, lady!" Tanner heard the man shout, and as he glanced to his left, he saw her stand up and draw her arm back and immediately knew who it was and what she was doing. He jumped out of his seat, popping Suki onto the ground, where, startled, she promptly squatted and peed. But it didn't matter. He had to take two long strides over there to keep that obviously still-aggressive Zoey Richards from giving the man she was with a bloody nose. He grabbed her from behind and pulled her into him, securing her left arm, thinking that would be enough to stop her from attacking.

But he clearly didn't know how tenacious she was. She merely twisted around and turned her other arm on him, her fist making contact with his cheekbone, whatever sharp ring she had on pressing hard against his flesh. Goddamn, she had a strong arm. And she was a hell of little wildcat, she was.

By then, another guy had come over and grabbed her

44

arms. Tanner kept her tight to him, her back spooned up to his belly. And even though she'd slugged him again, he became instantly and acutely aware of that pert little ass he'd glanced at before leaving the exam room, and how it was pressed against his cock, which was showing its appreciation by growing hard and proud, right up against the cheeks of her ass. She'd have to be clueless not to notice what the proximity of her body was doing to his.

And he had to be acutely aware that he was sporting a hard-on courtesy of the one woman in the world he would never, ever, ever dream of having sex with.

He needed to turn her around, pronto, before he came right there in his pants. He reached for her other hand as if she were a dance partner and twisted her around so they were pressed chest to chest, which frankly didn't help matters with him.

Her eyes grew large as she recognized who he was. "Dr. Eliasson!"

He grabbed both wrists to prevent any further injury and held onto them tightly. "Ms. Richards. I see you've made quite an impression on the place already."

She squirmed, trying to get out of his grip, then used a self-defense maneuver to extricate her hands from his clutches. "Look, it's not what you think. This man was harassing me. I was trying to eat my meal in peace and he kept demanding I give him his seat back, but it wasn't his seat; it was an empty chair. And this has been the worst day of my life, which is saying something, considering my fiancé left me for four other women, I've been abandoned by my shitty parents, and some idiot rammed my car, injuring my cat *and* my transmission. And now I have no place to sleep unless I hide in a tent overnight in the Great Outdoors Wilderness Shop."

They were so close he could see her eyes welling with tears. God, he was a sucker for a woman who cried. He wanted to make it all better. Even when the woman was someone who'd made *him* cry.

He did what came naturally, and pressed her head to his chest while she unleashed a chain of sobs that could have called forth the dead.

"There, there," he said, stroking her sexy hair, wanting to keep that stroke going all the way down her back and along the contours of her heart-shaped ass. Make that he wanted to in a general sort of way, not in a "with her" kind of way. Because, well, no way! This woman was about as off-limits as off-limits could be.

The thing is, Tanner knew he was cursed with this unstoppable need to rescue damsels in distress. So much so that he'd worked hard to redirect his efforts toward saving animals because it never turned out well when he rescued girls. As evidenced by that time he tried to help Zoey Richards out when she was a girl. Look at what that got him? A bloody nose and a reputation as a weenie. He needed to come up with a new hobby.

Whether he was chivalrous or merely a complete sucker, he could not leave a weeping woman without trying to help solve her problem. And he could solve this one with ease: he had rooms to spare; he could easily offer her up a place to sleep for the night, so the poor thing wasn't left sleeping on the hardwood floor of the outdoors shop. Even though he had to give her props for creativity with that notion.

"Look," he said. "I feel somewhat responsible for your being stuck here in Bristol tonight. Why don't you come back to my place? I've got plenty of room for you." He couldn't believe his mouth was betraying him. After he'd been so darned certain he'd dodged the mortar fire.

Zoey lifted her head off his chest and gazed into his eyes. "You have no idea how you've made my day, Dr. Eliasson. I owe you for this."

Oh, yeah. She'd owe him and he'd make her pay up: by getting the hell out of Bristol the minute he freed up ole Snowball in the morning.

Chapter Nine

ZOEY couldn't believe her good luck. Her day had turned from complete shit to, well, not complete shit, with the simple act of kindness from the handsome veterinarian. She'd expect nothing less from someone who cared for animals for a living. Surely they were a nicer breed than the rest of humanity.

It didn't hurt that he was super easy on the eyes too. His blue eyes seemed to pull her in yet also seemed to be holding secrets, which intrigued her. Plus he was fit, strong, and filled out in all the right places. And for the time being, she'd pretend she hadn't noticed that he'd started filling out in the right place, when her ass was pressed up to his pelvis. She figured she couldn't call him out on that because, well, she had been about to punch that obnoxious guy, and the good vet did rescue her before she landed herself in jail for the night. There was no question that his place would beat out the county jail's cramped cot and cold, hard, stainless steel toilet, hands down.

Although it was a little awkward going back to this man's house considering she didn't know him at all. And she'd left a slightly bleeding red mark on his cheek when her ring hit his face by accident. Thank goodness he had that cute puppy along—she was certain no serial killers ever kept a Labrador retriever puppy as a pet, so she knew she'd be safe. How was that for telling yourself what you wanted to believe?

As they walked to his parked car, he was silent. She kept up a running dialogue with the puppy, telling her what a good girl she was and cooing over how cute she was. When they got to his truck, he opened the door for her and offered his hand to help her climb up into the passenger seat. With an assist from her dad, Suki hopped in right onto Zoey's lap, which made her giggle.

"I feel a little better about letting Snowball loose in my car, seeing that you let your dog do the same," she said as she scratched the dog's head.

He shook his head. "Actually I seat belt her in most of the time." He pointed to a webbed strap that had been tossed on the floor of the truck. "But you were there, so…"

Zoey blushed. Now she was endangering the life of his puppy. "I'm sorry. If you'd rather latch her in?" Which sounded stupid because where would he put her? On the roof rack, where people out here would load up the dead deer after a day of hunting?

"We're not far from my place. But don't let me get into any head-on collisions. Or fender benders." He smiled.

She grinned back at him. "Yeah, I might not be the best person for that, but I'll do my best."

The long driveway leading up to his house was lined on either side with cottonwood trees. The property was fragrant with the scent from nearby pine trees, and as they approached a clearing, they passed a field with wildflowers of every color: pink and purple and yellow and blue. Zoey gasped, and he turned to look at her.

"Everything okay?" he asked, tilting his head.

Her eyes were wide open. "More than okay." She spread her arms out. "This. It's truly spectacular."

Not only were there amazing smells and beautiful flora,

but his home, a contemporary-looking log cabin that was hardly a cabin, was nestled in a pocket of land surrounded by the jagged, majestic peaks of the Rocky Mountains. The sun cast long shadows and threw shades of tangerine and melon across the landscape as it crept toward the horizon, preparing to go to sleep for the night.

Tanner nodded. "My little slice of heaven." His mouth turned up in a grin on one side and it took Zoey's breath away. He was quite a handsome man, what with that tousled blond hair, his sly grin, and those magnetic eyes. She found him to be most intriguing.

"You lived here a long time?" she asked.

"Long enough," he said.

Okay then.

"How 'bout you?" He pressed the garage door opener. "You from far away?"

"Far enough." She winked. Two could play that game.

"Fair enough." He winked back.

He parked the car and got out, coming around to let Suki out and then Zoey and reaching for her suitcase. Tanner followed his pup out into the yard and Zoey trailed after them. Suki found a tennis ball and brought it to Tanner, who threw it for her repeatedly and she brought it back readily.

"She's a good retriever," Zoey said.

"It kind of comes with the territory."

"Well, I had a Lab one time and she would never bring back anything I threw her. So I think the name is deceptive."

He smiled. "I'll grant you that. This one"—he pointed at Suki—"she's a smart dog. Hardly have to teach her anything twice and she follows along."

Zoey couldn't help but wonder if she'd been a Labrador, maybe her parents would've liked her more. As long as she did whatever they said…

After a vigorous game of fetch, they went inside his sprawling log cabin. The interior was a wide-open space that was warm yet masculine, with buttery leather sofas topped with Turkish kilim pillows in shades of red and orange, all surrounding a large glass-topped oak coffee table.

The living room had a large light fixture suspended from the ceiling that appeared to be made from the cast-iron sign at the entrance of a ranch, with pendant lights hanging from either side. The dining room featured a large farm table that could easily seat ten, paired with armchairs covered in cowhide. Looked gorgeous, if itchy. Above it was a chandelier made of animal horns of some sort—Zoey didn't want to know what type. One entire wall was a large stone hearth. Two walls were all windows, bringing nature inside, whatever the weather was outside. It looked like his own personal ski lodge.

Scattered throughout were all sorts of puppy toys. Clearly Suki had the run of the place.

"Nice place you have here, Dr. Eliasson." She nodded as she took in the entirety of the large space. "Thanks again for your generosity."

He shrugged. "Not a problem. It's the least I could do, holding your cat hostage and all."

"Well, I won't trouble you," she said. "You can go on about your business and I'll settle in once you show me to my room."

He shook his head. "Of course. How could I forget?" He grabbed her bag and led her down a hallway to a cozy room with a queen-sized bed piled high with a fluffy down comforter and plenty of throw pillows. "Once you get settled in, come back to the kitchen and I can get you a drink."

Zoey took a few minutes to throw water on her face— after a day of traveling she felt grimy and worn out. She brushed her teeth and finger-combed her hair, then returned to the great room, where the doctor stood in nothing but a pair of those outdoor hiking shorts that dry off quickly. She was afraid she might need to tuck her tongue back in her mouth upon seeing his tanned, muscular chest, covered with a smattering of light-colored hair. She wasn't sure which view she admired more—him or the mountains set against a twilight sky right past him through the wall of windows.

"So rude of me—I forgot to offer—if you'd like to join me in the hot tub—"

"I'd love to, but I don't have a suit with me."

He clasped his hands together. "Not a problem. Let me see if I can dig something up for you. Give me a few minutes." He held up a finger. "In the meantime, you can start on this." He handed her a glass of white wine.

Things were improving by the minute.

The doctor disappeared down the same hallway where her room was and she decided it was a perfect time to do some snooping. After all, the only thing she knew about the guy was that he was cute and had an adorable puppy. She didn't even know his first name. She walked toward a built-in bookcase and inspected the spines of books, looking for a clue about this mystery host of hers. Plenty of suspense novels from the usual authors, and a handful of veterinary manuals, but nothing too telling besides that.

Then her eye caught a photo album. Jackpot. She pulled it down from the shelf and opened it, rifling through pages of photographs of what appeared have been a younger Dr. Eliasson in college probably. She flipped back several more pages, until she came to a shot that looked all too familiar to her. That of the infamous boy she'd decked all those years ago. But how weird—why would he have a picture of him too? She looked at the boy's eyes, the shape of his brow, the clench of his jaw and wondered. She flipped ahead to more contemporary pictures of him and sure enough, it had to have been him.

Holy shit. Could it be possible that she was standing in the house of the Weeping Wimp? What was his name again? Tanner Cox? Impossible. This man here's last name was Eliasson. Probably a strange coincidence. Maybe he's a cousin or something.

She heard the floor creaking behind her and suddenly the vet came up right behind her.

"Find anything interesting?"

Chapter Ten

TANNER knew a lot about cats, particularly that adage about how curiosity killed one. And damn if that wasn't what had happened, only it killed him instead. Figuratively speaking. Here he thought he could maintain his anonymity, and instead Zoey Richards had to go and snoop and possibly even figure out who he was.

"The funny thing is I realized I didn't even know your first name," she said. "So, I thought I'd see if I could find something that would indicate who you are." She turned a not unattractive shade of red, which made Tanner have the tiniest bit of empathy for her. "Sorry. I know that was so rude of me. But I found these photos, and you remind me of a boy I knew long ago."

"Yeah, well, I have a common face." He dangled a white tank top and a small pair of running shorts. "If you don't mind, they once belonged to a previous girlfriend who left them behind. I thought they might fit you."

She squinted at him as she took hold of the clothes. "Okay. Sure. Let me go change."

"I'll be out in the hot tub. Come on out when you're ready." He pointed toward the back deck. He gave a whistle and grabbed a bully stick off the counter for the pup and Suki followed at his feet.

He tossed the treat for Suki, who grabbed it and ran onto the deck to enjoy it as Tanner climbed into the hot tub.

Earlier in the night, he'd hoped to escape the hassles of the day in here, but now he wasn't sure if he was about to face all that and then some, with his childhood nemesis putting on Katie's running clothes to soak in his hot tub while wondering if he was who she probably thought he was.

Tanner took a swig of his beer and about choked on it when Zoey came out in Katie's skimpy outfit. Damn, it looked better on her than it ever looked on Katie. He tried not to stare, but it was impossible not to. He reached a hand out to help her into the hot tub as she set her glass on the edge and stepped in. She took a seat across from him, obviously keeping a polite distance. That worked to his advantage, enabling him to get a good, long look at her tits, which were pretty much on full display now that the white shirt had gotten wet. *Kawabunga.* She had a smokin' rack, and it conveniently rested on the surface of the warm water— the better for him to see them in all their glory.

God, what he would give to suck on those things. *He did not just think that thought.* Hell no. There would be no sucking, there would be no fucking. This woman was leaving in the morning and taking Snowball with her. Out of his life forever and ever, amen.

"So you mentioned these belonged to your old girlfriend," she said, pointing at her makeshift swimsuit while taking a sip of wine.

Tanner looked out on the mountain range. A moon was rising in the distance, full and bright. God he so didn't want to revisit Katie. It had taken everything out of him before. The tears and the begging when he broke it off with her. She promised she'd "do better." Which was a knife in the gut because there wasn't a "do better" to do. She was jealous of his animal patients. Never could he reconcile with this. Not only was that weird, it was thoroughly incompatible with who he was.

He heaved a sigh. "I was serious with a gal for a while." He took a drink of his beer. "It didn't work out."

"That seems obvious, considering I'm wearing her shorts and top." The shirt was bubbling up with the force of the water, so she gave it a tug down. Too bad. He was hoping for an even better view if it slipped right over the tops of those things.

"Yeah, well, we had different outlooks on life," he said. "She resented my spending time with my patients. It was like she was competing with them for my attention. For that matter, she didn't even like my patients."

She squinted at him. "Wait a minute." She brushed her fingers through her short hair. "She didn't like the animals that were your patients? How could you not like animals? Especially ones that are in need of medical care? She sounds a little heartless."

"Yeah, well, besides that, we'd seemed compatible. She loved the outdoors. We enjoyed a lot of the same activities."

"Well, I don't know you and it's none of my business, but you seem like a nice guy, so I'm glad you ditched her. You deserve better than that."

He smiled. That was a thoughtful thing for her to say. "Thank you. But enough about me. I seem to recall you saying something earlier about a wedding that went bust? Some fiancé who left you for *four* other women?" His eyes widened in incredulity.

Zoey covered her face with her hand. "Oh God. Did I actually blurt that out?"

He nodded. "'Fraid so."

"Don't suppose we can leave it at that?"

He shook his head. "Are you kidding? After you were snooping in my pictures and I spilled my guts to you about

Katie?" He tipped his beer can back and took a drink.

She stuck her lower lip out. "Katie. Such a perfect little name, isn't it? Katie. Like is there ever a girl named Katie who isn't perky and cute and bubbly and vivacious and girl-next-door and all that and a bag of chips?" She growled. "God, I hate all the Katies in the world. For being so fucking perfect and nothing ever goes wrong and they don't have zits when they're thirteen and they never get their periods when wearing white pants and they always have perfect parents and their cars don't get rear-ended and their fiancés would never gangbang behind your back—"

Tanner spit his beer out on that one and his eyes grew larger still.

"I'm sorry." He pretended to clean his ears out with his finger. "Did you just say, 'gangbang behind your back'?"

She nodded. "I found all these group messages from these women he was having sex with at some swap club or something."

He smiled. "For clarification, I think you didn't mean gangbanging. In case you ever told anyone else that. Because that would imply sexual assault."

She held her hand to her mouth. "Oh, crap. I can't even get my accusations against the guy right. So what is the proper terminology—gang orgy?"

"I'm gonna be honest with you here," he said, sliding a little closer to her, thinking he might have a crier on his hands any minute. "I am so not up on my group sex jargon, and I don't want to steer you wrong. But yeah, I'd say any word with the term 'orgy' in it would work under the circumstances."

"See—Katie would never have had this experience."

"By Katie do you mean my Katie? Or random Katies throughout the world?"

Zoey tapped her nose with her forefinger. "Bingo. Any old run-of-the-mill Katie would never lose her fiancé to a bunch of skanks like that."

Tanner suppressed a laugh. "Would you hate me if I started cracking up? Because while your story is indeed tragic, your delivery, well, you gotta admit, it's pretty damned funny."

She heaved a sigh. "Yeah, well, if you can't laugh, you cry, right?"

"So this fiancé of yours—did you know each other for long?"

She covered her eyes then peered through the slits between her fingers. "You're really gonna think a lot of me when I tell you no. I met him on vacation in the Dominican Republican. He was cute. He saved my life. We got on like a house on fire. He was hung like a horse, and well, the rest is history."

Tanner held up his hands in a "T." "Wait a minute," he said. "Time out. I'm not even sure where to begin. He saved your life?"

"In a manner of speaking," she said. "More like he guarded my life."

"What, did he continue to apply SPF 30 so you didn't burn?"

"No, silly. He was my jump partner when I went skydiving in the DR."

"And he saved your life how?"

"Because we were attached together for the jump. It was up to him to be sure I didn't die."

"Okay, I guess I'm following you. Ish." He laid his head back on the edge of the hot tub and stared up into the darkening sky. "And the horse bit?"

"What horse bit?"

"You said he was hung like a horse."

"Oh God. Did I say that?"

Tanner nodded.

"I'm giving it all away tonight, aren't I?"

"And you can't leave me hanging now. Excuse the pun." He grinned at her.

"So I was a little overwhelmed by how he protected me and I guess I mistook that for intimacy and well, we celebrated after the jump and things sort of followed from there."

And it matters that he was well-endowed?" He shifted in his seat. "I've always wanted to ask this of a woman. *Does* it matter that much? Or is that all about the guy's ego?"

She pursed her lips. "Promise you won't think less of me?" She seemed to worry about this often.

He dragged his finger over his heart in an X. "Swear it."

"Pinky swear?"

She leaned toward him, reaching her pinky out for him to link his with. It gave him a chance to peer down her shirt and finally, he got an honest-to-God peek at her nipples, pink and swollen. He was most grateful she couldn't see his cock coming to immediate attention beneath the bubbling water.

"It's way better with a guy who's got it going on down there. It happens to be the truth."

Tanner breathed a sigh of relief, safe in the knowledge he'd been bestowed with a cock that many women had gushed over. He'd been curious about whether that mattered to her. It was kind of fun getting her to spill her guts like this.

"Can I ask how you went from skydiving to engaged to the guy? I mean a big cock can only get you so far in life."

It was Zoey's turn to laugh. "If that's not the understatement of the year." She high-fived him. "Then again, his big cock got him to LA, then got him engaged, then got him at least four women at one time at the Greater Los Angeles Swappers Club."

"There isn't such a thing, is there?"

She frowned. "'Fraid so. In fact, if you call right now, you'll probably be able to reach Rodrigo and his stable of skanky women there."

They both laughed.

"So did you truly love him?"

She shrugged. "Looking back, I think I was in love with being in love. I don't want to get too deep here, but I'm not sure I ever knew what love was. I kind of grew up in a loveless household, and I'm afraid I equated lust or a sense of security or something like that with love. I feel stupid saying that now, but the good news is we'll never see each other again, so I might as well share all my secrets with you."

Tanner smiled. "You know what? I can't think of someone I'd rather hear her deepest, craziest secrets from." He clinked his beer to her wineglass.

And he meant it. Which was not a good sign. Because he was steering clear of this one. No two ways about it.

Chapter Eleven

ZOEY was on her third glass of wine and her head was swimming in a good way. She was having fun in the hot tub with the hot doc. Well, veterinarian. Which she supposed was still a doctor. Like Doctor Doolittle.

"Doctor Doolittle, I presume?" she said, a slight slur to her voice.

Tanner raised an eyebrow.

"Does anyone call you that?"

"Not that I know of."

"Well, I suppose I can see why I'd have thought of it. After all, you *do* a *lot*. Get it?" She'd somehow moved closer to him what with all the vigorous motion of the bubbles, so she was able to lean in and elbow him jokingly in the ribs over her stupid joke, only her forearm grazed what she had to presume was a wicked big hard-on lurking beneath the surface of the water. *Dayum.* If that wasn't tempting, nothing was. But no, she'd already had her one-night-stand-with-a-stranger, and look where that got her.

Actually it got her right here, right now. Were it not for that little lapse in judgment, she'd still be sitting in her parents' Malibu cottage, hating that she was sitting in her parents' Malibu cottage. So much for that argument. Nevertheless, she didn't even know Dr. Doolittle, though he seemed nice enough, and he didn't know her, except he knew all about her disastrous love life of late, which was mildly embarrassing. Then again, it felt good to get it out there. After a lifetime of having to live the veneered life of a child with celebrity parents, it was liberating not to give a shit who knew what about you. No secrets, no pretense, simply calling it like it was.

Huh. On the one hand, that would be the most perfect time to sleep with someone, wouldn't it? One of those completely zipless fucks—no muss, no fuss, a lot of fun because you enjoy each other's company, but no interest in anything more than that. A drive-by fuck.

She forgot why she'd become so focused on the sex she was not about to have with Dr. Doolittle, and it made her a bit sad she wasn't going to have it. Because, well, it was evident he had the hots for her. And sure, she found him quite handsome and interesting. What would be so wrong with two people indulging a little?

Ugh, she'd done that with Rodrigo, hadn't she? And that experiment failed miserably.

But the thing is, sometimes when you're a little lubricated up with a few glasses of scrumptious wine, you act on impulse. And the fact was, Zoey's mother always berated her for her impulsivity, whether it was scaling a palm tree in her bare feet on some island in the South Pacific while she was on a shoot, or jumping off someone's balcony into their swimming pool below, or yeah, getting engaged to the skydiving version of a glorified cabana boy.

But then she started thinking about that swollen cock that had pressed against her arm and she was intrigued. Maybe a teensy bit of fun would be okay? Like not the whole thing but enough to tide her over till she found a new guy for real? A little bit of fooling around in a hot tub? After all, isn't that what hot tubs were invented for? What the hell. Nothing ventured, nothing gained.

She leaned into the doctor's personal space only a smidge.

"I've been dying to do this—would you mind terribly if I indulged this one time?" she said, angling her head and pressing her mouth to his, her tongue probing for signs of compliance. He opened his mouth immediately, and her tongue began exploring along his lips, his teeth, his tongue. This guy was a way better kisser than Rodrigo, and that was saying something.

He reached around and pulled her toward him, and she let out a groan of pleasure. As their bodies met, his hard cock pressed up to her pelvis and she couldn't help herself; she reached down and stroked the head through his shorts. It was his turn to groan this time as he clasped her face between his hands, securing her in place to deepen the kiss.

Good God, this was an out-of-body encounter of the best kind. How this day turned into this night was a complete mystery but in the best sense of the word. When she thought it couldn't get any better, the doctor began to kiss along the edge of her jaw, his mouth moving toward her neck, drawing his tongue along the column of her throat. And she could feel things stirring down deep she hadn't even felt when Rodrigo was at his best.

With ease, he reached into the scoop-necked edge of her T-shirt and lifted both breasts above the fabric, allowing easy access to each one. He pressed them together, and nipped at first one nipple, then the other, before his mouth closed over one nipple and he pulled hard. Yowza, if he kept that up, Zoey would climax long before anything more ever came of this little tête-à-tête.

Oh, but the idea of coming made her think this was too much like having sex and honestly, she needed to maintain at least a scintilla of integrity with herself at this point. Hadn't she promised herself no one-nighters? This was beginning to have all the hallmarks of a one-nighter, and she knew she'd end up mad at herself afterward. But, man, that tongue, dragging across that nipple, those teeth taking the occasional friendly bite of one or the other. Meanwhile she'd been stroking his cock and if his breathing was any indication, he was into it. As he rocked his pelvis toward her hand, it felt so good. How could something so good be so wrong?

Willpower. She needed to prove to herself she had some. So even though she was fast approaching orgasm, she had to stop this. Otherwise his hands might find their way down her shorts and there'd be no question about orgasming once or even twice before they were through. Inevitably, certain hard things would end up inside certain soft things, and that spelled trouble for Zoey. So instead of indulging in the feelings, which were freaking amazing, she pulled back. Her nipple slipped from his mouth with a soft pop.

Dr. Eliasson's brow wrinkled. Even more so when Zoey let go of his cock, midstroke.

She held up her hands as if under arrest. "I'm, I'm, I'm super sorry about this," she stuttered out of nervousness. "Believe me, this is the last thing I want to do. But I promised myself no more one-night stands. That's how I got engaged to Rodrigo—with stupid, impulsive actions on my part that might have been fun but were terribly consequential."

He frowned. "Okay…" He drew out the word for a few beats. "I'm totally on board with whatever you want as long as you're sure about it. I mean, whatever that just was, was a whole lot of fun. You're sure you don't want to maybe keep going for a little while longer?"

She nodded, worrying that all he'd have had to do was say "pretty please with sugar on top" and she'd have folded like a piece of origami paper. "I know. And I feel bad about it. But I mean, look, in the middle of all this, with my hand on your erection—and honestly, I was a bit relieved when I felt it because I thought you might be teensy weensy, what with your concern about that earlier—I thought, 'Well, I don't even know this man's first name.' I should at least know the name of the man who I'm masturbating."

"I think it's only masturbating when you're doing it to yourself."

She squinted. "Really? You sure about that?"

He nodded.

"Okay, the man who's dick is in my hand. How's that?"

He smiled. He must've thought she was crazy. Maybe she was.

"So anyhow, I'm grateful for your hospitality tonight. And for Katie's makeshift swim gear. I'm sure you're happy about that too since you could see through it pretty easily once it got wet."

He cocked an eyebrow. "You knew?"

She nodded. "Can't say I didn't enjoy the tease a bit. And when my arm hit your cock by accident, well, I knew it was working."

He thrust out his lower lip. "You're a hundred percent sure about this, then?"

She nodded, hanging her head. "I'm afraid so. It was fun, but I'd forgotten, I'm turning over a new leaf. A new, one-night-stand-free leaf."

With that, she stepped out of the hot tub, pulled off her wet top only enough to squeeze the excess water from it and maybe cause his jaw to drop, tugged it back on, and started walking into the house.

"Tanner," he said loud enough for her to hear it once she'd entered through the door. "My first name's Tanner."

As she walked down the hall, she closed her eyes against the sneaking suspicion that was gnawing at her. There was no way this guy was that Tanner. No doubt there were plenty of Tanners in the world. Of that, she could be sure.

Chapter Twelve

I had her nipple in my mouth and she pulled it out. Tanner couldn't get that out of his mind. Why, oh why, would she *foreplayus interruptus* like that? Was he not doing a good enough job? Talk about an ego blow, if that was the case, although it was hard to imagine. She seemed as into it as he was. With the exception that she was able to restrain herself, and he could no sooner have voluntarily stopped his momentum at that point than if the house had caught fire. Maybe he should recognize this as his lucky break. He, too, had no plans to do what they were doing. Sure it was a lot of fun. And knowing what he knew now, he'd dive right back into the hot tub if given the chance. But what a mistake that would be.

How had it even started? He'd been ogling those tits all night. It would have been downright unfair if he hadn't had a chance to get his mouth on them before the night was over. Although he was in clear violation of Tanner's rule of chastity number one: don't stare at a woman's tits if you don't want to get turned on. And he had been crazy turned on.

When her elbow grazed over his erection, he'd damn near jumped out of his skin it was so electric. The next thing he knew, her tongue was in his mouth and it seemed as natural as a baby taking its first steps. He couldn't believe he'd hit the jackpot like that. Yet now here he was revisiting the whole thing in the shower as he jacked off, doing to himself exactly what she'd said she was doing to him. Same act, different actor. He kept trying to decide if he'd screwed up somewhere to drive her away like that, but no. What was he supposed to do—turn the woman down? Think how that would have made her feel. Besides, imagine how awkward the silence that would have ensued under those circumstances.

He closed his eyes as the warm water sluiced down his body, his slick hand stroking the length of his cock. It didn't help matters to replay the why's. He needed to think about the what's: the way her tongue felt sliding alongside his and tracing the contours of his mouth as he did hers. And her hands grazing along his abdomen and that moment right before she slid her fingers beneath his shorts to clasp his hard dick with both hands, working them in concert to drive him crazy. In his fantasy, she eventually worked her way down his body, her tongue and teeth trailing a lazy pathway to his cock. And then her warm, wet mouth circled the head of his dick, teasing the crown as he thrust himself deeper into her mouth. He imagined the suction her mouth made as she pulled him in and toward her throat. So warm. So wet. So hungry for him.

Which was all it took right there in the shower for him to stiffen, every nerve synapse in his body redirecting its focus to his cock as his balls tightened and his come spurted onto his belly, mixing with the warm water that showered down on him.

It was nowhere near the experience it could have been if she were here with him, but at least now he'd get some sleep and not obsess about the woman sleeping—naked? Would she be stark naked?—a few doors away from him.

Suki had him up with first light, so he headed off for a brisk morning hike with her, leaving a note behind for Zoey, so she didn't think he'd deserted her. After hiking for about an hour, he stopped on his way back through town and grabbed two coffees and a few pastries. He entered the kitchen through the garage door, balancing one coffee atop the other as he kicked the door shut with his foot. He set the drinks and bag with pastries on the counter and turned to see Zoey coming down the hall. She had hair sticking up in all directions and half-moons of yesterday's mascara beneath her eyes.

"Good morning, sunshine," he said, making his voice as cheery as possible, so she didn't feel uncomfortable about how things were left last night. No sense in making it worse than it was.

She nodded. "Is it, though?"

He squinted. "Well, yeah, I'd say so." He pointed outside. "The sun is shining. It's a lovely, cool temperature. Suki and I took an amazing hike. And I brought you coffee and pastries." He held out a coffee cup. "I left it black, just in case."

She clasped it in two hands and held the steaming cup toward her face. "Thank you so much for making me human again."

"You mean last night, or now?"

She threw him a side-eye. "About last night—"

He held up a hand to stop her from elaborating. "Nothing to say. It was a mistake on both of our parts. You're going to be on your way very shortly, our paths never

to cross again. It was wise of you to nip that in the bud."
Nip. As in *nipple.* As in even he didn't believe what he'd said.
It was incredibly stupid to have stopped that train barreling
down the orgasm track.

"About being on my way shortly—" She looked up at
him with the big brown puppy dog eyes, and he knew there
was a problem. He crossed his arms over his chest, bracing
himself for whatever bad news was coming his way.

"I talked to Garth."

"The mechanic?"

"Yeah, him," she said. "And he said there's another
problem and he's got to order another part, so it's going to
be at least another day till my car is ready, maybe more."

"At least?"

She crossed her arms in a dueling body language battle.
"What can I say? It's out of my hands." She held up a hand.
"But seriously, I'll figure something out. Surely there must
be a rental car place around here. I'll find a car, then I'll drive
to the nearest town and I can stay there until the car is
ready."

"The closest town with a hotel's gonna be about an
hour south of Banff."

"Are you kidding me?"

"Believe me, I wouldn't lie about something like this.
Montana is the land of wide-open spaces."

"Isn't that Texas?"

He shrugged. "It's probably everything between the
West Coast and the East Coast. But I'm certain you'll be
mostly to your destination before finding a place."

"Okay, that's good. It's like four hours there, right? I'll
find a place up there and relax for a day or two. After all, I'm
in no hurry."

"What would you do with Snowball?"

"She'll be fine. I've got the cat carrier. I've got her food. I've got her litter box. I'm sure there's a hotel there I could stay in."

"Not one that allows cats."

She rolled her eyes. "Why is there such a bias against cats?"

He laughed. "First off, cats don't want to be lugged around from place to place to begin with. Secondly, cats have a lot of dander and people are allergic. They can't have a hotel room that's going to give people hives."

She closed her eyes as if lost in thought. "I don't know what else to do."

"Don't be ridiculous, Zoey," he said, his arms still crossed over his chest. "Of course you're welcome to stay here as long as possible."

"But what about Snowball?"

"Snowball can have the run of the place."

"You mean she can come here? With me?"

He nodded. "I'll swing by the office and grab her and some cat supplies, litter, a litter box and stuff, and we can get her set up."

"What about Suki?"

"Suki will welcome her with open paws."

She looked up at him with her wet brown eyes. "You sure about this?"

"Positive."

Yet the only thing he was positive about was that it would be positively impossible to keep his hands off this woman, who even looked sexy in her little cotton pajama shorts set, with her hair sticking out all over the place. He was so screwed.

Chapter Thirteen

GOD forbid Zoey minded her own business while Tanner went off to retrieve her cat for her. Nooo… Instead she took advantage of his absence to do more snooping. Somehow in the heat of the moment last night, she didn't ever find a way to ask him about the whole mystery of the boy in the photo album. Not that the opportunity presented itself. She'd chosen to route things in another direction. She had yet to figure out a way to do this delicately. Not like she'd blurt it out and say, "Are you the same person I punched in the face when we were kids?" If he was that boy, he sure was trying to steer clear of the topic. Although maybe he hadn't a clue who she was. Except he knew her name. And she now knew his: Tanner. But not Tanner Cox. Why would that be?

She returned to the photo album and pulled it down, going back to the page with the pictures of the boy who looked quite like the boy she slugged. She slipped the photo from the sleeve and flipped it to the back. "Me and Mom on the set of Dad's film *Wildcat*, 1999" it said in sloppy kid's printing. That would put it at the right timing. It was probably a year or so later that she'd had her fateful encounters with him. He sure looked like it. And it was on a film set. Who else could it be?

She quickly stuck the picture back and flipped forward to another page and saw irrefutable proof. It was a photograph of young Tanner, sitting next to the swimming pool with his dog Sunshine. It even said it on the back: "Me and Sunshine taking a swim, 2000." That was the very pool where she and Tanner saw all the grown-ups. Jesus. What a small freaking world it was.

Back when this happened, to say Zoey was scarred was an understatement. She loved to pretend she was a sassy, sophisticated nine-year-old, but in fact, she was about as worldly as a toad in a pond. She knew grown-ups had their times when they didn't want kids around, but she figured it was because they were discussing work or something. Not because they were going to be naked and do all sorts of nasty things right in front of everyone. In front of their prying children's eyes.

As an adult, she could zoom out a little and see it from adult eyes as perhaps not quite so skeevish. Not that she was going to do something like that, but she realized that some people did. Take, for instance, her former fiancé's behavior, which ought to have made her all the angrier. Until now she hadn't even drawn the parallel. She laughed, imagining Rodrigo at some swank party up in the Hollywood Hills where everyone was stripping naked. He, of course, would win the whole night hands down what with that horse appendage that he could practically swing like a baseball bat. Probably intimidate all the men in attendance. And certainly it had made four women swoon. The bitches. But she thought it had comic potential as well. Like what about the caterers? Were they naked too? Or did they circulate through the party with drink trays and passed appetizers, offering up canapés to people with no pockets to stuff the disgusting caviar appetizer in once they realized what it was.

Yes, it was creepy that her parents were doing that stuff. But at the time it felt like the rug had been pulled out from under her. Sure, she knew her parents made her a low priority, and often she was a prop for their successful careers, someone to drag out and put on display to make them look better. But still, they were her parents. And, she figured, for the most part, they were normal and did normal things that would not include gallivanting around a cocktail party stark naked with your hands on another person's body. Hell, she hadn't even known her parents did that to *each other* at that point.

With so many years having passed, she could cut her parents some slack over their betrayal, at least when it came to this. But the overall fact that they sucked as parents? Not so much. So when she'd packed and ran last week, she'd meant it. She was over trying to forge a tepid relationship on their terms with people who didn't care much about who she was as a person. As she stood in Tanner's living room and assessed the situation, she realized she was officially on her own.

The good news? She had a fat trust fund that would always make her financial life comfortable. But as far as her personal life? She'd lost her fiancé and her parents all in the span of a week. It made a girl feel awfully alone in the world. Then again, sometimes when you take down large, dead limbs from an old tree, you realize how much more sunshine can get through. So maybe she needed to start seeing things through a different lens.

All of a sudden, she felt a cold puppy nose on her thigh, and she turned to see Suki and Suki's dad standing before her. One was wagging a tail, one wearing a frown as she stood there looking guilty and foolish with a photograph of young Tanner and Sunshine in her hand.

"Uh, sorry, I realized when I was looking at your pictures last night I forgot to put one back in the sleeve, Dr. Eliasson."

He reached for the photograph in her hands and took it from her, dragged it along the length of his pointer finger as if it were a playing card, then weirdly changed the subject. "If we're going to be cohabitating, you're going to need to call me by name."

Huh. What a strange response to busting her spying in his photo albums. But she was going to go with it and see where it led them.

She lifted an eyebrow. "Which I was wondering about."

"You were wondering about my name?"

"Well, sort of," she said, her toe scuffing the hardwood flooring. "More like who you are."

"I think you know who I am."

"But do I?"

He nodded. "I'm Tanner Eliasson. I'm the vet who cared for your cat after your fender bender."

"But who are you really?" He glared at her. Well, shoot. That wasn't the response she was hoping for. "I mean, well, does the name Tanner Cox ring any bells for you?" He turned away from her and started to straighten out the magazines from the nearby coffee table. She followed him, standing right behind him. "Because I think it does."

Chapter Fourteen

SHE couldn't leave it alone. Bad enough she ruined things for Tanner once. Now she had to do it again? What the fuck?

"Look, Tanner," she said, placing her hand on his shoulder to turn him toward her.

He held up his hands and pointed toward the door. "Your cat is over there. I need to... do something."

With that, he stormed out of the room, down the hall, and into his bedroom. He was spitting mad and didn't want to say something he'd regret.

But once he was in his room, he couldn't stop pacing back and forth, dragging his fingers through his hair. He should've stayed at the office. It was his day off, although things were busy enough in there they could have used an extra hand. But no. He came back thinking it would be nice to entertain his unexpected houseguest. Only to find her sticking her nose where it decidedly did not belong.

He sat down on the bed and reached for the remote and turned on the TV. Perhaps he could drown himself in a baseball game or something to escape this quagmire. Unfortunately the first channel he turned to was airing *The Beast Within*, of all the damned things, starring none other than Alexa and Armando Lipari. They played two star-crossed lovers, separated when Armando's character is wrongfully sent to prison for ten years, where he then marries another woman, played by Gina LeFevre, who fell in love with him after writing him letters of support in prison.

Jesus, could he not get a break from this blast from the past? And by blast he meant of the nuclear variety. He threw the remote against the wall and heard the clatter as the batteries fell out. Sprawled across the bed for a while, he tried to figure out what exactly had him so angry—was it her snooping? Was it her finally blowing a cover he'd protected for so long? Was it his crap parents, rearing their ugly heads even now? Was it the fact that ESPN wasn't the first thing that came on when he turned on the television?

He heard a soft knock on the door, then the creak of the doorknob. Suki nudged her head in, then jumped up against the bed, her paws reaching out for her dad, not quite tall enough to hop onto the bed unassisted. He looked over to see Zoey hoisting the pup up onto the bed. Should he even mention that he didn't allow her on the furniture? He let Suki lavish his face with kisses until she curled up in a ball at the foot of the bed. Oh, she was gonna hear it later on for her misbehavior, but he didn't have it in him to kick her off now.

"Why don't you want me to know that you're Tanner Cox?" Zoey asked quietly. He could barely hear her over the noise of his mom and her dad panting and grasping at each other as they made love in a conjugal visit scene in the film. If that wasn't enough to turn him off of sex forever, nothing was.

"I don't even know what you're talking about."

"I think you do. You and I spent a night together—"

"I've never slept with you."

She sat down next to him on the bed. "I didn't say we slept together. I said we spent a night together."

He knew, and he was sure she knew, that had she not

stopped things last night, they'd have certainly spent the night together last night.

"Look. I know you're Tanner Cox. What I can't figure out is why you're going to such great lengths not to admit it."

She looked up at the screen where their parents were canoodling and rolled her eyes, then pointed at the screen. "Really?" She shook her head.

Tanner was so mad he wasn't sure what to say. "I'm going to start calling you Blurt."

"What do you mean, Blurt?"

"Because on a regular basis you blurt out things that make no sense and it makes me crazy trying to decipher your crazy talk."

"What are you talking about?"

He waved his hand dismissively. "This ridiculous nonsense you're saying right now. It's crazy talk."

"You're telling me you're not Tanner Cox?"

He fumbled on the bed for the remote, but came up empty-handed.

Zoey went over to the floor where it lay with batteries now missing. She got down on her hands and knees and padded around until she found them. Standing up, she reinserted the batteries, handing the remote to Tanner. He thrust it toward the screen with far more force than was called for, trying to change the channel. But it wouldn't change. Instead they were left to listen to the gasps and groans of their parents in the clutches of high-def ecstasy.

Zoey sat down on the bed, facing Tanner. Suki looked up and thumped her tail a few times, then lay back down, thoroughly disinterested. Zoey waved her hands in front of Tanner's face. "Hello! Paging Tanner Cox. Come out, come out, wherever you are."

He swatted at her hand. "Stop calling me that."

"Fine, I'll be glad to as soon as you explain what the heck is your deal?"

Tanner heaved a sigh. "Jesus, Zoey. Can't you leave things alone?"

"What things?"

"This." He splayed his hands as if there was something specific before them he was referring to. "That." He pointed to the television. "Us." He aimed his finger at her and then at himself.

"But why?"

"Christ. Why must there be a reason? Because I said so. Do you have any idea what I've had to do to shed the skin from my former life? Do you know how shitty it was to be Tanner Cox? No thanks to you, I might add."

A rush of red crawled up Zoey's neck and spread across her face. "Look, Tanner. That was so long ago. Why are you still concerned about something that happened a lifetime ago?"

"Because it ruined my life, that's why."

Zoey's lip started to tremble. "It ruined your life?"

He nodded, staring straight at the television screen, refusing to look in her direction. He could hear her voice beginning to quake and he was determined not to cave and help her feel at all better for what she'd done to him. "Yes. It fucking ruined my life. Here I was this dopey, lonely, gangly kid. I already didn't have many friends. I was freeze-framed in my parent's bogus, superficial *Access Hollywood* life, and they were mostly not even there regardless of the bullshit perfect life they portrayed to the public. Bad enough I couldn't do anything about it. And then I go to that stupid movie premiere and some girl—*you!*—pulls back and coldcocks me, for no reason whatsoever." He took a deep breath. "Do you have any idea what it means to be a ten-year-old boy who is shamed for being a wimp, a sad-sack loser?"

Zoey started to cry, a quiet sob. "I had no idea," she said, her voice cracking. "Honest, I didn't. It was all so awful, I can't even remember much about the whole thing. I remember my mother made me dress up in this awful frock and I didn't want to go, but they made me and all of a sudden there are your parents and there are my parents and there you were and you had been there with me at the swimming pool and saw everything I saw. It was more than I could bear to deal with—"

"I was there, yeah. Only because you made me go. I told you we couldn't go to the pool, yet you made me take you to the pool. We would have been blanketed in blissful ignorance if you'd have simply listened to me. It wasn't my fault you saw that!"

"You should've put your foot down and said no. That would have been the chivalrous thing to do!"

"Chivalrous? Are you crazy? I did put my foot down and say no! Besides, I was a fucking child. You were peer pressuring me and I stupidly caved to your demands." He growled, combing his fingers through his messed-up hair. "Honestly, this is why I moved far away from people like you."

"People like me? What's that supposed to mean?"

"You know exactly what that means. People like you who traumatize people like me."

"I didn't mean to traumatize you. I was traumatized. I didn't know how to process everything. It scared me. I didn't mean to do anything to you that night. I don't know, I guess I panicked. And your face got in the way of my freak-out."

He turned away from the television and glared at her.

"Yeah, my face happened to jump out in front of your fist."

"You have to believe me—it wasn't about you. It was about me."

"But like it or not, it became all about me. Overnight I was the butt of jokes all over the world. They did a fucking skit about it on *Saturday Night Live*, for crying out loud. They tried desperately to book me on all the damned morning shows and even the stupid *Tonight Show*. My parents tried to make me appear on them! You think a kid that age is not going to be mercilessly teased by every kid in school after being 'beaten up' by a little girl? It took years for this to go away, for me to finally scrub the sordid Tanner Cox legacy off my skin."

"Oh, Tanner, I hate that I did that to you. I had no idea how hard I made your life. I feel absolutely awful about it."

"And then you come parading in here after I open my doors to you, a complete stranger, and you have to pick open the scab."

"I promise, I didn't even know who you were. I dug around because I was worried you might be a serial killer and I was looking for proof you were a normal person."

"That explains last night with your snooping. Doesn't satisfy your having done it this morning."

"Well, sure it does. Last night I found out not only were you normal, but you were someone from my past. Who wouldn't admit to it. I needed proof of it."

"So you could resurrect all the shit I went through?"

She shook her head, tears leaking from her eyes. "I didn't think it through, Tanner. I guess I was curious."

"Remember that cat that was killed by curiosity?" He frowned. "Speaking of, where's Snowball?"

"I left her in my room to get acclimated."

"You sure she'll be okay in there? Sometimes cats don't

take to being left alone in tight quarters at a strange place."

She waved her hand. "She's fine." She reached for the hem of her dress to dab at the tears still coming down her face, giving Tanner a peek at her black lacy panties. He was a guy, after all—a little emotional trauma wasn't going to stop him fantasizing a bit.

"The thing is, after all that happened, I was so humiliated. Girls laughed at me. Guys mocked me and called me a pussy and beat me up. I was treated like a pariah. If I didn't have friends before, I sure didn't have them afterward." He scrubbed his hands across his face. "I hated my life. I hated being the only child of two narcissistic Hollywood celebrities. I counted the minutes until I could get the hell out from under their thumbs. And then I did it. I made a clean break. I got away. I carved a new life for me. I left Tanner Cox behind, thrilled to be done with that part of my life. I moved on. And I never looked back. I've never once had to deal with all the fallout from that since I walked away from it. And now this." He glared at her.

She squinted at him. "Did you know it was me when I walked into your exam room?"

He shrugged. "Sort of hard not to with your name. And I could still see the little girl Zoey in your face. Your big brown eyes. Your dimples. Like it or not, I remembered these things about you because, well, let's say you left a lasting impression on my life."

"And still you took me in?"

He extended his hands palms up. "What was I going to do? Let you get into a fistfight in a bar and hauled off to jail? Or leave you to sleep in a tent in the store? That would've been sort of shitty of me."

She shook her head. "Dammit!"

He furrowed his brows and leaned over on the bed.

"What?"

"Now I'm remembering. That night. When my folks dumped me on you. You were so damned nice to me. Took me in, offered to play Legos. Took me to get food in the kitchen. And all I did was cause trouble."

"I kind of remember you telling me trouble was your middle name."

She started crying again. "I used to say that, jokingly. But you know what? I did that to deflect the pain from hearing it from my mother all the time. One of her many ways to make me feel bad about myself."

Tanner leaned forward and brushed some hair away from her eyes.

"I remember something else you told me too."

She lifted a brow. "Oh yeah? What?"

"'Get comfortable with being uncomfortable.' I remember you saying that to me and I thought it was a smart thing for a little kid to say." He combed his fingers through her cropped hair. "Little did I know it would need to become my motto shortly thereafter."

"I suck."

"You don't suck. You were a brave little girl and you got scared. Maybe you got a little too uncomfortable." He reached for her hand and laced his fingers with hers. "You know what my motto was?"

She shrugged.

"Stay under the radar."

She half laughed. "Well, looks like you finally managed to do that at least."

"Yeah, but yours is far more courageous than mine."

"I guess sometimes I can be a little too bold."

"Like when you leaned over and kissed me last night?"

She nodded. "Maybe like that."

Skirt Chaser

"So how brave would I be if I leaned over and did this?"

Chapter Fifteen

IT was a surprise gesture, especially considering Tanner was pointed in one direction at the top of the bed and Zoey was aimed in the other, her legs hanging off the edge. Somehow Tanner managed to twist himself around and pulled Zoey's body toward his, then pressed his lips to hers. She was sure her heart skipped several beats at the unexpectedly sweet gesture. Here she was expecting him to repay her with at least harsh words—because no self-respecting man was going to punch a woman, so that couldn't be on his agenda even though she deserved it—and instead he kissed her. And the kiss was soft and tender and sweet and lovely.

He reached down to Zoey's bottom and pressed her center to his hips as he rolled on top of her and ground his pelvis to hers, making it abundantly clear that while his intentions started out sweet, they were rapidly moving toward sexy.

"I can't believe you stopped this cold turkey last night." Tanner breathed the words into her ear as he caressed the cheeks of her ass.

"It was one of the stupider things I've done in my life," she said, panting. Boy was it ever. What was she thinking, stopping the train in the middle of the tracks like that?

"In which case, I think we can both agree we need to make up for lost time." He shifted up her sundress and slipped a hand beneath the edge of her panties, his fingers quickly finding her wet and needy. Zoey thrust her hips toward his fingers, reaching for what she knew he could give her. She let out a moan.

"Christ, Zoey, you know how much you kill me?" Tanner said as he swirled his fingers through her juices, then pressed two fingers inside her, his thumb playing with her clit. Meanwhile his other hand pulled the neckline away from her dress and deftly lowered the cup of her bra, exposing a breast. He promptly settled his mouth over her nipple, sucking and biting like a starving man. The pleasure reached deep into her pelvis, right where the beginnings of a climax were taking shape. She spread her legs wide, giving him better access as she pulsed her hips in time with the rhythm of his hand movements. Jesus this felt amazing.

Between what he was doing between her legs and the way his mouth worked in masterful ways at her breast, Zoey knew she was about to explode. And when Tanner picked up the pace of his fingers, slicking through her moisture, she began to moan.

"Oh God, Tanner, don't stop. I'm going to co—" She didn't even get the rest of the sentence out of her mouth as powerful spasms racked their way through her pelvis, reverberating throughout her body. Starbursts of light sparked behind her closed eyes. It took her a minute to settle down and collect her breath.

"Remind me why I put a stop to that last night?"

Tanner shrugged. "Hell if I know. But now we have to make up for lost time, remember?" He shifted himself down her body and Zoey protested.

"Oh, no. Uh-uh, Tanner. No way can I come again so quickly."

But he ignored her and continued kissing his way down her belly, his fingers on one hand plucking at a nipple while the fingers of his other hand pulled the edge of her panty leg out of the way to give him room to work his magical tongue. And it *was* magical. As Tanner continued to play with her nipple, his tongue traced the soaking wet seam of her center, lapping at her juices and circling her swollen clit. Soon Zoey's breath came hard and fast and her hips pressed to his mouth as her hand held his head where she needed it to be. She reached for her other nipple and pinched at it.

Tanner paused to watch her contribute to her own pleasure. "Shit, that's so freaking hot," he said, returning his focus to her pussy. While he licked and sucked on her, she pressed her foot against the swell in his pants—he still had his clothes on for goodness' sake. She did her best to pleasure him, but with much of her body preoccupied with what he was doing to her, it didn't last long. She felt another low rumble in her belly and she squeezed her nipple hard, helping him do the same with his other hand as she thrust her pussy to his mouth. And soon, she felt the convulsions of her climax tightening and loosening in wave upon wave of pleasure, till at last, her pulse settled down and she stopped, gasping for air.

"That tongue of yours should be a registered weapon." She winked at him as she pulled him toward her, leaning over to lick her juices from his face.

"The better to pleasure you with, my dear."

"Is that like 'Why grandmother, what a big tongue you have!' Only you're the big bad wolf?"

They both laughed. But not for long, because Zoey wanted to get down to business and reciprocate Tanner's generosity. As her tongue lapped at the juices on his lips, she slid her fingers down and unbuttoned his shorts, quickly lowering them off his hips. She shifted her body, slowly crawling downward as her mouth explored his throat, chest, nipples, and taut belly. When she got to the trail of hair, that happy little road sign sending her due south toward her goal, she tugged his boxer briefs down, pulling them off. And she kissed and licked her way to his hardened cock, that beautiful, thick, long cock she never got to thoroughly acquaint herself with last night.

Zoey grasped it in one hand and licked the swollen tip like it was a lollipop, circling her tongue around the rim, then dragging her tongue across the sensitive tip. She circled her fingers at the base of his cock, stroking him upward as she sucked and took him deep into her own mouth. Her other hand moved farther down to cup his balls, lightly toying with them. He let out a long moan.

Tanner ran his fingers through her hair, pressing her head to accept as much of his cock as possible, and she was more than willing to do so, taking him deep down her throat. His balls retracted, his body tensed, and she tasted his salty precum seeping from the tip of his cock.

"Christ, babe. I'm gonna come," he said as he thrust hard and his body stilled, before releasing wave after wave of his seed into her mouth.

It was then that Zoey realized she'd done precisely what she swore she wasn't going to do with Tanner Eliasson/Cox. Or was it to Tanner Eliasson's cock?

Shit. She was hopeless. She couldn't keep her panties up or her expectations down, and now she was going to pay the price for that. Because in the short time she'd been around this new, improved version of the childhood Tanner, the nice kid whose heart she erroneously broke because of her bad behavior, she realized she was falling for him, like a meteor dropping out of the sky, sure to burn something upon impact.

Chapter Sixteen

TANNER was hit with such intense postorgasm exhaustion that he must've slept for about a year.

When he eventually turned over and looked at the clock, it was more like half an hour. And he was alone in his bed, no Zoey to be found. Even Suki was missing in action.

He got up, took a quick shower to rinse off, slung a towel low over his hips, and went in search of the Miracle Mouth. Because damn, she'd done some incredible things with that mouth and he needed to make sure there would be a command performance in the near future.

He walked across the hall and down one door and quietly knocked on her bedroom door.

"Go away," she said.

Huh? They'd just had this amazing makeup, well, foreplay, and she was already sending him packing?

"Zo—can't I please come in?"

"We'll talk later. I need some time to think."

Well, shoot. Never a good thing when a woman has a sexual encounter with a man, only to shut him out within minutes because she needs to think. Who thinks after sex? Not that they officially consummated things, but still. Christ, the only thinking going on in his brain was reliving how fucking amazing her mouth felt on his cock. And what a turn-on it was when she came in his mouth. And when he came in hers.

He scrubbed his hand over his face. He needed to see her and not let her apprehensions—or whatever this was—fester till they became debilitating. Because whatever they'd experienced was about the best thing to ever come out of his entire upbringing, and he didn't want to immediately ruin such a good thing.

He knew it violated some sort of post-almost-coital code of conduct, but he did it anyhow—gently twisting the handle to the bedroom door, slowly opening the door, and peering in. What looked to be complete vandalism had taken place in there.

"What the hell?"

"Tanner! I told you I didn't want you to come in."

He shook his head. "I know, but I didn't want you getting all freaked out by what happened. Little did I know you were way more freaked out than I assumed."

She gave him the side-eye. "It wasn't me, Tanner. It was Snowball. I mean, maybe I'm freaking out too, but this—" She pointed to the room's down comforter, which had been shredded by cat's claws, with feathers still floating through the room. "Argh! I'm so sorry. I'll pay you back for it."

He shook his head, squeezing the bridge of his nose between his thumb and forefinger. "Man, the subversive power of an angry pussy." He wondered which pussy he was talking about.

"Yeah, well, better this than our flesh."

He nodded. "So true. But I think she's telling you she wasn't happy being locked in this bedroom."

"Yeah, but what was I to do? I didn't want her to ruin your whole house."

"I tell you what. Why don't we get out of the house for the rest of the day? We'll take Suki with us so that Snowball can feel more at home, and she'll have a chance to settle in without anyone upsetting her sensibilities."

Zoey wrinkled her brow. "What if she does this to the whole house?"

"If you'd feel better, I can give her a mild sedative. It wouldn't have any adverse side effects, and it should help reduce her stress. She'll probably sleep the whole time we're gone."

She frowned. "You're sure it won't hurt her?"

"I promise. Your pussy is in good hands with me." He grinned. "Or at least it was a little while ago."

She heaved a sigh. "About that—"

Tanner held his hands up. "No discussions right now. Let me get dressed and run over to the office to get some medication for her. You'll need a bathing suit unless you want to wear Katie's outfit again." He smiled but got no reaction from her. "Would it help if I swung by the mechanic's and grabbed whatever else you might need from your car?"

She nodded, stroking her scared kitty cat, and Tanner couldn't help but wonder what had Zoey so fearful. At least she wasn't likely to tear his place apart while he was gone, although he got the sense she was likely to take a wrecking ball to the sexual attraction between them that sizzled like droplets of water on a hot griddle, and like it or not, he had no way to stop it. Once again, it all came down to what Zoey Richards did.

Chapter Seventeen

ZOEY couldn't abide the awkward silence that had descended over them as Tanner navigated his truck through some rough back roads on their way to what he told her was his favorite hideaway—a swimming hole with a natural thermal spring that he'd discovered awhile back on a long hike one day. He'd figured out a way to drive much closer to it so they wouldn't have to hike in since Zoey didn't even have a pair of tennis shoes along. She wasn't going to make it far with a pair of flip-flops if they had to hike for two hours to get there.

The silence was her fault; he was seemingly on a postclimax high when she shut him down after the whole Snowball debacle. She felt so conflicted about everything. First she was mad at herself for not sticking to her guns. And she was mad at herself for being mad at herself. After all, they'd had a fun time, so what was the harm? Then she was mad at herself for being mad at him even though she wasn't actually mad at him. But since he thought she was, that made her feel bad.

Sometimes it was hard to be a fickle female. She needed to somehow stir up a conversation—yet she wasn't that person who could stand in an elevator with one other person and not have words. Especially when the silence was all her fault.

She pulled out her phone and started checking out

pictures on her Instagram account, but that made things worse. It seemed like everyone had pictures of themselves with a significant other being happy together: at picnics, in a bar, in bed first thing in the morning, doing yoga. God, she hated those women who did death-defying yoga poses hoisted upon the twenty-five-inch-biceped arms of some male supermodel boyfriend of the month. Like who does that stuff? No normal male she'd ever encountered would partake of such activity unless they were part of a circus troupe or it was some freaky foreplay.

Making a mental note to stop looking at Instagram when she felt like shit about her personal life, she decided to text Izzy to see what she was up to.

"Busy Izzy, what is going on, sister?" She added a smiley emoticon for good measure.

"Zo! You never called me when you got in!"

"That's because I'm still not in. I got stuck in this little cow town in the middle of Montana," she said. "It's sort of cute, looks like the Hollywood version of the Wild Wild West. A lot of horse-themed motifs."

"It's just like riding a horse."

"Speaking of riding a horse—"

"Please tell me you did it with some guy on horseback."

"????????????????"

"I'm serious. It sounds so intriguing. Some couple in a book I read did it on horseback and it sounded sexy, but I always wondered if it was far more trouble than it was worth."

"Not to mention scratchy. And dangerous. Can you imagine falling off a horse, naked, with horsehair rash on your ass? Nothing about that sounds even remotely appealing to me."

"Yeah, but with the motion of the horse walking, that

would move the guy's cock inside in a rhythmic way."

"Honestly where do you come up with this stuff?"

"I told you, it was in a book."

"I gotta ask you where you get your reading list from."

"I think my mother told me about it."

Zoey shook her head. "See, that's the thing. Can you imagine my mother suggesting an erotic book with people having sex on four-legged animals?"

"Knowing your mom, it would be people having sex with four-legged animals."

"Ewwww." Zoey attached a vomit emoji to that one.

"Sorry. I was joking. But trying to get the point across that your mother is a bitch."

"Mission accomplished."

"So, tell me what is going on that made you get stuck in Montana? Even though I can think of worse places to be stuck."

"Some woman rear-ended me, and poor Snowball got thrown into the front seat. I had to find a veterinarian to check her out, and then my car is messed up and they can't get the parts, so I'm stuck here."

"Oh no! How's my kitty doing?"

"She's fine, just a little freaked out by the whole thing." She added three white kitten emojis for reassurance.

"Thank goodness. Precious cargo on board."

"Aren't you gonna ask about me?"

"Oh, goodness. Sorry 'bout that. How are you?"

"Fine. No harm done to me, only my car. But I am itching to get out of here and up to Banff."

"Well, hmmm… Just so you know, I'm heading up there in a few days."

"To Banff?"

Izzy sent her a whole line of heart emojis.

"Does this mean you're planning to go to your place and have sex twenty-four seven with the guy from HR?"

"The thought had crossed my mind."

"Does this also mean I'm uninvited now?"

"I wouldn't say that." Izzy typed. "It's more like I wanted to give you a heads-up that we would be there, in case that made you uncomfortable."

"I'm gonna hear everything, aren't I?"

She sent a shrugging hands emoji. "The walls are awfully thin."

"Annnnd you couldn't do it on the kitchen counter either."

"How'd you know that was my plan?"

"Izzy, Izzy, Izzy. How long have we been friends?"

So crap. This threw a big wrench into things. By the time her car was done, she'd no longer have a place to stay in Banff. At least one that didn't sound like the Mustang Ranch Brothel on a busy holiday weekend. And Lord only knew how long it would be until Izzy and her new man were sexually sated enough to return to LA. At the rate she was going, that could be months.

"To change the subject, what're you doing in this cow town to keep busy? And how's my surrogate kitty, Snowball, faring being stuck there?"

"Snowball flipped her shit and destroyed an expensive duvet, so that was bad."

"What'd the hotel say about it?"

"Not staying at a hotel."

"Where are you staying?"

"With the veterinarian."

"?????????"

"It's a really long, really weird, really complicated story."

It didn't take ten seconds for Zoey's phone to ring. She

switched the sound off and let it go to voice mail.

"I'm not in a place where I can talk," she typed.

"I know you work fast, Zo, but this seems like world-record fast. Please don't tell me this guy's moving back to LA with you."

Zoey rolled her eyes. She makes one big mistake and will she ever live it down?

"Yeah. He found five women who want to bang him."

Izzy sent emojis of five women in bikinis with a laughing-face emoji.

"Very funny, Iz. But this is serious."

"With this guy? Please tell me you're kidding me."

"No. There is no relationship with this guy. Well, there was. Oh, never mind, that's complicated. But what I'm dealing with is serious. I need your advice."

"Cryptic much? Fire away."

Against her better judgment, Zoey filled her friend in on the whole story, from the punch twenty years ago to what happened this morning.

"Holy shit, Zo."

"Tell me about it."

"So what do you want me to say?"

"I want you to tell me what I should do."

"Can I tell you what I would do?"

"Same difference."

"Well, then that makes it easy. I'd go for it. You're stuck there for a few days. You might as well make it as enjoyable as possible. Consider it like a must-see tourist attraction."

Zoey burst out laughing. Tanner looked over at her, arching his eyebrow. She shook her head and held up her phone so he knew she was engrossed in a more important conversation via text messaging than she'd been with him. Nice message to send the guy after all he'd done for her.

Hell, he hadn't even charged her for Snowball's medical care.

"You are a sick woman, Isabelle Strong."

"Only trying to give you a different perspective. I mean you can say your house burned down or you can say you now have a chance for a whole new house. It's all in how you look at it."

"So you're telling me it's perfectly fine if I fool around with Tanner, and it's no reflection on me being impulsive or irresponsible or anything like that?"

"I mean it could be, but honestly, Zoey, who cares? It's your life. Wear it proudly. So you messed up with Rodrigo. I'm sure you learned some lessons from him too. So maybe it came out a net positive."

"Yeah, I learned that I like doing it with a guy with a big dick."

"I can't tell you how badly I wish I had a big dick emoji right now."

Zoey smiled. It was nice to have a friend you could have a ridiculous conversation with like this: no judging, no anything but a friend being a friend.

"So, Tanner, eh? It's a good name. I picture a guy named Tanner would have sexy wrists."

"WTF does that even mean?"

"You know, when a guy rolls up his sleeves, and you look at his wrists, and there's that perfect amount of hair on them, and usually he's got a big watch on, and, oh, I don't know, it looks so fucking sexy. If your name is Tanner, you're much more likely to have those wrists."

Zoey surreptitiously glanced over at Tanner's arms, which were tan and strong and yeah, quite sexy. He had hands that looked so capable. And she'd already learned how capable they were. But not only with her, where it counted most, but even with Snowball. How he held her close to his chest and gently pried open her mouth and slipped that pill in and how he stroked her throat to encourage her to swallow it. This after Snowball had scratched him till he bled, then shredded his down comforter.

"I think you're onto something with that wrist thing."

"See, I told you."

"So what am I supposed to do? It's like I let the horse out of the barn. Now what?"

"You know what I'd say to that."

"?"

"I'd tell you to mount your man on that steed. And report back to me if it actually works in real life or if that is merely a fantastical plot point in a novel."

Zoey burst out laughing. Tanner looked at her, one side of his mouth curving into a smile.

"I've gotta go see a man about a horse, Iz. Thanks for the advice."

Chapter Eighteen

TANNER had no idea how he was supposed to act. Here he thought it would be a fun day out with Zoey, but her mood had turned dark and her cat had gone temporarily insane, which upset her even more. This outing seemed to be a practice in awkwardness. Once they got to the hot springs, maybe he'd take Suki out on a hike and leave Moody Mona to herself.

What was she doing on that phone? Every couple of minutes she'd burst out laughing. He liked her laugh. It was sort of loud and bawdy—the type of laugh you'd hear from a beer wench in a pirate pub.

There must be some way to break the ice or break through the iceberg. Not that he hadn't already broken the ice, but somehow the thaw had ended and he wasn't sure how to get back to where they'd been. He sucked at figuring out women. They left him scratching his head half the time. Heaving a sigh, he looked over at Zoey as she tucked her phone back into her purse.

"I'm still wondering," she said. Finally! Actual words from her mouth. "When you figured out who I was, why didn't you say anything to me?"

"Because I couldn't wait to get rid of you. If I had struck up a conversation, it would have ended up an emotional archeological dig for those bones… those rotten, desiccated bones that were buried deep in my psyche. The last thing I wanted was to return to that old graveyard. So I couldn't wait for you to leave."

"Is it safe to say you hated me?"

Tanner turned to stare at her. "Hate is an awfully strong word, don't you think?"

"You hated me, didn't you?"

"I don't hate you now. And I didn't know who you were. I mean I knew who you were, but I didn't know *you*. I knew what you'd done, the Rube Goldberg machine you set in motion, the steel ball at the top of the roller coaster, ready to knock down all the dominoes in its wake, oblivious to the chaos it was unleashing."

"You make me sound so unpleasant."

"I didn't mean to," Tanner said, lifting his hands off the steering wheel in exasperation. "I was trying to convey how I felt."

"Like I was human hazmat."

"Why do I get the feeling this conversation is only going to go further off the rails? Look, I thought you were hot. And we've had some fun, but let's be real. This can never go any further. Me? With the girl who made my childhood unbearable?"

He cringed at the thought of all it evoked in his memory.

Zoey was silent.

"We'll be there in a few minutes. Then you can relax and pretend I'm not there. Suki and I will take a hike, literally, and leave you at peace."

He turned down a narrow dirt path, barely wide enough to fit his car, and after a couple hundred yards, they came to a clearing. He put his car in park, got out, and came around and opened the door for Zoey and Suki. He gave Zoey his hand to help her down; instead, she held onto the doorframe. Okay, then.

Tanner spread his arms out. "So this is my secret getaway. Warm water, even warmer rocks to lie on, and a view to die for." He handed her a towel. "You can spread out on this if you don't want to lie right on the rocks, and all I ask is you wait to swim till I'm back. Fair enough?"

Zoey nodded. No doubt she was more than happy to unwind all by herself with a book and no Tanner.

Tanner grabbed Suki's leash and the two of them followed a path where they soon got swallowed up by overgrowth so that Zoey could no longer see where they were. She spread out her towel and slathered lotion onto her back and shoulders and legs as best she could, then lay down, first untying her bikini top to avoid tan lines. She read for a while and even drifted off to sleep. She woke with a start, fumbling for her phone so she could check the time. It had slid down the rock a bit, so she sat up, reaching for it as she heard Suki come charging through the brush, barking and wagging her tail. Topless Zoey grabbed hold of her phone and raced to grab her bikini top, only to see it dangling from Suki's mouth. *Noooo!*

"Suki! Come!" she shouted, lowering her voice to sound alpha to no avail. She decided to make a quick break for it, chasing Suki before Tanner emerged from the woods to see her half-naked. Not that he hadn't already. But she was still smarting from his admissions about her. She was in no mood to expose herself to him either physically or emotionally.

She thought she had Suki and the bikini top cornered near a thicket of nearby trees, but that dog was too fast for her and dove right when she dove left. Dammit. She regained her footing before she went face-first (and it would also have been boob-first) onto a gravelly area of soil. But it left her clumsily running and leaning forward, her tits bouncing happily around like cow's udders. It would have been terribly embarrassing for Tanner to have seen that.

When she came to a stop, narrowly saving herself from near disaster, she learned too late that Tanner had been watching all this unfold. She was certain he'd orchestrated the whole thing to see her tits bouncing around. He stood before her, arms crossed across his chest, hips shoulder distance apart in a Superman pose, a shit-eating grin pasted across his face, no doubt enjoying the free show.

Zoey stood facing him, impulsively covering each breast with the palm of a hand. As if that was called for at this point.

Tanner lifted his eyebrow and half smiled. The darned dog danced around her feet, dodging Zoey's attempt to reach down for the top while trying to cover both breasts with her forearm and hand. It was hopeless. Eventually Suki lost interest in Zoey's clothing and dropped it, most inconveniently at Tanner's feet.

"Good girl, Suk," he said, pulling a cookie from his pocket and making her sit before handing it to her. He picked up the bikini top and pretended to inspect it while Zoey stood there, her hands still trying to do business as a makeshift bikini top.

"I don't suppose there's any point in my politely asking you to hand me that, is there?"

Tanner scratched his head. "What's it worth to you?"

"Huh. What's my dignity worth to me?"

"No need to be so bashful, Zo. You know I've seen them before."

She gave him her best "no duh" look, complete with snarled lip.

Tanner started to slowly pace back and forth, his gaze fixed on hers. "For that matter, I've sucked on those pert nipples before."

She rolled her eyes. As if she didn't already remember how amazing that felt.

"In fact, I had the distinct pleasure of watching you play with those nipples yourself. Do you remember?"

Listening to him talk dirty to her like this was making her wet. She had no idea she loved to hear a guy recount what he'd done to her sexually and decided to tuck that information away for future encounters.

"So what say we make a little deal," Tanner said as he pulled his shirt over his head. "And I'll even things up so you don't feel like you're the only topless one here."

Zoey stared at his muscular chest, his cut abs, that crazy sexy "V" where his shorts slung low on his hips, a giant man-billboard advertising what awaited the next lucky girl to follow the yellow brick road. It was the guy equivalent of a titty bar sign's flashing lights that read "Girls! Girls! Girls!" Zoey knew what lurked right beneath that one little snap and zipper. And she knew it could easily become her happy place. She crossed her legs against the throbbing she felt as her clit engorged with blood. Jesus, this guy made her react in all sorts of out-of-character ways. Like in any other universe, she'd be screaming for her bikini top, demanding that he give it back. But she loved the way she could feel him undressing her with his eyes. Even though she was already mostly undressed, but for a skimpy bikini bottom.

"I want you to squeeze those nipples between your thumb and forefinger, Zoey," he said, fixing her with an intensely sexual stare. "I want—I need to watch you play with yourself. You know how much that turned me on to see you doing that this morning?"

She nodded, somehow suddenly held captive beneath his erotic spell.

"Will you do that for me, Zo?"

She slid her palms down, leaving only her thumbs and pointer fingers at her breasts. And slowly she grazed her fingers over the tips, around the areola, even the slightest touch shooting straight to her clit, which made her cross and uncross her legs as she tried to satiate the need to touch there too.

"It's okay, Zo. You can put your fingers there too." Tanner nodded his head as he looked at her crotch. "Can you see how hard I am watching you pleasure yourself?"

She glanced down to see he was indeed hard, the outline of his erection pressing against his shorts.

"In fact, I'll make a deal with you." His hands reached to the button of his shorts and he easily unfastened it, then began to slide the zipper down. Before she knew it, his shorts were at his ankles, followed by his boxer briefs, and before her stood the most glorious cock she'd ever had the pleasure of meeting: right there, clearly pleased with Zoey's pleasuring herself. Tanner wrapped his fingers around his cock, ever so slowly fisting his hand up and down, making the tip of it swell even more and turn a deep red.

"Go on, Zo," he said, pointing to her bikini bottoms. "Just slide your fingers beneath that waistband."

Keeping one hand on a nipple, Zoey complied. At last, she could satisfy the growing need to slick her fingers through her wet lips, swirling them around her swollen clit, doing what she could to bring her to that peak she needed so desperately.

"That's it, Zoey," he said, locking eyes with her as his strokes grew more intense and he spread his legs enough to reach down to grab his balls too. "It feels good, doesn't it, babe?"

She nodded, her breathing now at a staccato pace, her breasts heaving as she too spread her legs to make it easier to trace her fingers along her highly sensitized labia, then slide her fingers inside her. She moaned out loud.

"Come for me, Zoey," he said. "And keep your eyes on mine."

It was like he was some sort of sexual Svengali; she was unable to not do as he said. Nor would she want to defy him. It felt far too good. The climax took hold, an electric bolt of pleasure that began in her clit, or was it right where she'd squeezed her nipple hard? Or was it deep down in her pelvis, or maybe when she slid a third finger up inside of her? It all splintered everywhere at once, a crescendo of lightning zapping through her body as her legs grew weak from the effort, tremors turned to convulsions, and finally shudders as her heartbeat slowed. Even as she came, she'd kept her eyes fixed on Tanner's, but now she looked down to see his cock an angry, swollen red, and she knew the one thing it needed. She crooked her finger and Tanner cocked an eyebrow as she nodded in assent. She padded toward a rock, peeled off her bikini bottoms, spread her legs, and bent forward, leaning her hands against the rock for support.

Zoey turned around and looked over her shoulder at him.

"Well? What are you waiting for?"

Chapter Nineteen

TANNER had to pinch himself to be certain he wasn't dreaming this, although he couldn't have even concocted this in his wildest of dreams. And he sure as hell wasn't going to give Zoey a chance to change her mind, so he made time getting from where he stood, dick in hand, to where she stood, dripping pussy in waiting.

She was ready for him, and he grabbed her hips with one hand as he lined up his cock with her notch. He must've been a Boy Scout in a previous life because he had to do the courteous thing and double-check with her.

"You sure about this?"

"One hundred percent, but the longer you wait to slide your dick in me, the greater the chance I'm going to rethink this, so hurry the hell up already."

He took a deep breath. "Talk dirty to me, baby," he said as her tight, slick pussy pulled his cock inward. He groaned. "That feels so fucking amazing, Zoey."

Once he was seated deep inside her, he clutched her hips, pulling her toward him, going in even farther. His breath came in spurts, and he tried to savor the moment but needed to feel the glide, the in and out, the walls of her pussy closing in around the head of his cock as it swallowed him up. Pulling almost all the way out, with the tip of his dick still inside her, he plunged hard, increasing the pace as he thrust deep, then pulled out, pumping his hips in sync with the arch of her back and gaining even better access.

He reached around with one hand and found her swollen clit and began to circle it with his finger. His other hand inched toward her breast, where he played with her nipple, pinching and pulling and caressing it all while he continued to drive his cock deep inside of her. The orgasm was building in his balls, at the base of his cock, her pussy milking it out of him.

"Come with me, Zoey," he said as he stilled, buried deep inside her, and emptied himself inside Zoey Richards, the woman he foolishly thought he'd never want to see again. And when she shouted out his name, then trembled as her climax coursed its way through her body, he knew that was the craziest concept he was never more glad to cast aside. Because he couldn't imagine not doing this, with her, at least for the indefinite future. He was falling hard for Zoey Richards, and all of a sudden he was good with that.

"Race you to the water," Tanner said, giving Zoey a playful slap on the bottom as he got up and sprinted to the water's edge. They'd napped in the sun after that unexpected little playtime and now he was refreshed and ready to go.

As he'd lain on the hot rock with Zoey tucked into the crook of his arm, he thought it might be awfully easy to get used to this. He imagined the two of them making it a regular thing, heading out to the hot spring. Maybe they'd even hike to it, bring camping equipment, and stay the weekend. He could take Zoey up to the edge of the cliff where he and Suki had hiked earlier in the day. The view from there was spectacular, looking down toward a pristine blue lake that was a popular hiking destination. There was so much to share with her and the idea of doing that excited him.

Tanner took a running jump into the water, but Zoey took her good old time, strolling slowly toward the water's edge, stark naked, which was fine by him: he got his fill of the spectacular view as she strode, her sated body loose and content, right up to the edge. Preparing to do a cannonball, she jumped in and splashed him.

He laughed. "Oh, you naughty thing, you. You'll pay for that."

He swept his arm across the surface of the water, launching a splashing battle, with Zoey squealing as they horsed around in the water. All the commotion compelled Suki to get over her fear of jumping into the water and she leapt in to save them. She paddled around, sleek as a seal, while they laughed at how cute she was. After a bit, Suki took a rest on a nearby rock, and Tanner seized the moment to wrap his arms around Zoey in the warm water and pressed his lips to hers.

"Why, Dr. Eliasson, is that a dog toy in your pocket or are you just happy to see me?" Zoey said as she wrapped her legs around his waist. Tanner groaned as she pressed her center up against his burgeoning hard-on.

He nipped at her earlobe and whispered in her ear, "The good news is it's all for you if you want it."

"You know I want it," she said as she slid herself over his cock, back and forth, until the tip notched perfectly at her opening and he slid in. "Mmm… good."

"Good not great?" He kissed his way around her face.

"Well, I don't want you to get a swollen ego."

"To match my swollen cock?"

"Exactly. That's all I need, thanks."

Tanner secured his hands beneath her ass and helped

her lift and slide down onto him, the rhythm building as her nipples pressed against his chest. The sensation of their slick bodies rubbing together, skin on skin, was amazing. As the warmth of the water enveloped them, his lips tenderly nipped at hers. They linked mouths, their tongues mimicking the mating ritual that had them moaning into each other's mouths.

"I could get used to this," Tanner said between kisses, pressing his forehead to Zoey as he thrust hard into her warmth.

She sighed. "I don't know if we'd survive it."

"I'm a doctor. I'd make sure of it."

"You're an animal doctor."

"And I have animalistic lust for you, so it works out perfectly."

She laughed. "Shut up and fuck me, Dr. Eliasson."

"Tanner," he said, slamming hard into her.

"Fine. Fuck me hard, Tanner."

And he needed no further instructions. He buried his cock deep inside her and stiffened, his body racked with spasms as he unloaded into her and her pussy convulsed around him, milking every drop.

They stayed entwined in the shallow water, their breathing still heavy as they came down off their climaxes.

Tanner pulled back for a moment and extended his arms to her shoulders, taking a good look at her body.

"You know, I like this look even better than the one you had on last night."

"Yeah, generally naked is better."

He nodded. "I can't put a fine enough point on that sentence. In fact, I would opt to stay naked as often as possible with you if you'd let me."

"I could be persuaded, Dr. Eliasson. That's the

problem. I could be persuaded."

Chapter Twenty

A series of tents were being erected in the park when they got back into town.

"Oooh, what's going on here?" Zoey asked.

"It's the weekly farmers market," Tanner said. "You want to stop by?"

"It looks like fun. But"—she swept her arm across her body—"I probably look a wreck."

Tanner glanced over at her and grinned. "You look like a sexually sated woman who has been thoroughly fucked."

She smiled.

"Without doubt," she said. "But do you think everyone will notice?"

He grabbed her hand, lacing his fingers with hers. "So what if they do? They'll be jealous."

"That I've dug my claws into the hotly desirable Dr. Eliasson?"

He laughed. "Well, maybe that. But more like they'll be jealous of me that I got to bury myself deep inside of you."

"I had no idea how much I liked a man talking dirty to me until you." She stroked her thumb along the back of his hand. "But we'd better lay off that at least while we're wandering around the market. Don't want to give anyone ideas about what a horndog their local vet is."

He pulled her hand on top of his crotch, showing her how hard he'd gotten yet again. "As long as you keep this happy, it'll be our secret."

"I think I can agree to those terms."

Bristol was a small town, so it seemed everyone knew Tanner, which made Zoey feel like she was on display for the locals to appraise. She wished she'd had a chance to do her hair and maybe wash up a bit. After all, she'd spent the afternoon having sex with her new veterinarian. But she loved that she felt part of a couple as they wandered the stalls, tucked beneath Tanner's strong arm, Suki a few feet ahead of them, relishing attention from the puppy lovers in the crowd.

It was then that it dawned on Zoey: this felt right. Like nothing she'd ever felt before with another man. Like two pieces of a puzzle that fit together perfectly. What a shame that they had such different lives, different plans. There was no way this could last. She was moving on, and besides, Tanner didn't want to have any attachment to his past, and she was nothing if not a constant reminder of what he never wanted to remember.

It made her sad to realize this was going to come to an end. As soon as her car was fixed, she and Snowball would be on their way. There was no choice but to enjoy it while it lasted.

They passed by stalls that were selling all sorts of food, from barbecue to Thai food, as well as jewelry stands and all sorts of craft items. At a nearby set of chairs, a woman was offering foot massages and they stopped.

"Go ahead, Zo. She does amazing pressure point

massages."

"Really?" They certainly didn't have foot massages at the farmers markets she'd gone to in LA. But when in Rome…

Five minutes later, Zoey's eyes were rolling back in her head from the pleasure. She didn't want it to end.

Tanner leaned into her ear. "Your face looks the same as it does when you're about to come."

"That's because I am about to come," she whispered to him. She started laughing. It might not have been that pleasurable but it ran a close second. "Now you know the way to my heart."

He nodded. "I'll keep that in mind."

Next they passed by a fortune-teller. Madame Zorza, a fifty-something woman with a long gray braid and a crinkly smile in her warm, brown eyes, stood in a pair of Tevas with black capri leggings and a silk shawl draped over her shoulders, motioning for the couple to come inside her tent.

"I'm always a little scared of fortune-tellers," Zoey said.

"Oh, it's all silly. Completely harmless."

"What if they tell me something really bad is going to happen?"

"What if they tell you something really good is going to happen?"

"Will you act as my interpreter?"

"Is that legal with fortune-tellers?"

"Anything is legal. It's all silly, remember?"

"So what would my function be then?"

"You'll be my conduit. So she tells you my fortune and if it's good, you tell me, and if it's not, you keep it to yourself."

"But you'll know if it's not good and that'll bother you."

She shook her head. "I promise. I won't press you. I'll

let it be whatever it is."

"And you won't be mad at me if I don't tell you?"

She held up three fingers. "Scout's honor."

"You sure that's not two fingers?"

She shrugged. "I have no idea. But I'm good for my word."

"I have an idea," he said. "Regardless, I won't tell you here, now, while we're at the market. We'll agree on a set time when I'll reveal—or not reveal—your fortune."

She squinted at him, wondering if this was a good deal or not. "Hmmm…Trying to see a downside to this."

"The good news is it would preclude you punching her if it was bad news."

She curled her lip at him. "Ha-ha. Very funny."

He pointed to his face; it still bore a scratch from her near miss the other night, which made Zoey feel awful. Was that only last night when she'd accidentally kind of hit him? Good Lord. It seemed as if they'd been together for weeks.

Tanner pulled his wallet out and paid Madame Zorza thirty bucks and she closed the doors of the tent. They explained to her how this was going to work, this somewhat unconventional delivery system.

She held Zoey's hands in hers, palms up, and she began to trace the lines in her hands, talking about what they meant.

She then crooked her finger at Tanner, who was sitting in a metal folding chair between the two of them. He stood and walked to Madame Zorza, who leaned toward his ear, speaking behind her hand so Zoey couldn't hear what she was saying.

She spoke to him for about three minutes, with Tanner maintaining a stone face the entire time. Zoey took the opportunity to give Suki an ear rub, which made her thump her tail in joy.

"I know how you feel, girl," Zoey said. "Lucky you—you get massages as much as you want. After today, not me." She was a little wistful. All of the fun she was having with Tanner would soon draw to a close. And she had to figure out what to do if she couldn't go to Banff.

At last, Tanner stood up straight and dusted off his hands as if he'd finished an odd-job and had not just heard the fate of Zoey's life.

"Okay, Zoey," he said, his face revealing nothing about what the soothsayer had soothed. Or said. "Let's go."

Crap. This must be worse than she thought.

Chapter Twenty-One

"IS my leg going to fall off?"

Tanner shook his head. Zoey had been bugging him since yesterday about the findings of the fortune-teller. The thing is, they hadn't remembered to agree to a time for him to reveal—or not reveal—the prediction. And so he was left to try to process it while figuring out what to say to her and when. Listening to Madame Zorza had kind of freaked him out, and he had no idea how he was supposed to broach this with Zoey. So he'd remained cagey.

"Leprosy. I'm going to die an early death from leprosy. I knew it." She gave an overly dramatic tug to her hair. "God! Why did I agree to that stupid fortune-teller?"

"I can assure you there was no mention of death by leprosy, Zo." He chuckled. "Although she did say something about me possibly suffering death by nagging."

She swatted at him jokingly.

They'd been pleased upon their return last evening that Snowball had settled in surprisingly well. No more crazy destruction. And after a couple of swipes with claws extended at Suki, the kitty and the puppy seemed to have reached an agreement that the other didn't exist, which was better than there being a bloodbath had Suki decided she was a toy and had Snowball seen her as a sworn enemy to her species. Zoey had gotten a call about her car—it would be ready in the morning, which meant she and her cat would be gone soon. Any animal bonding at this point was irrelevant.

Tanner was surprised at how blue it made him, thinking that Zoey would be gone in twenty-four hours. Two days ago he would have paid good money to get rid of the woman. But it took her coming into his life to realize that she had nothing to do with anything bad in his life—rather he'd wrongfully vilified her all those years. Maybe he'd have been better off pursuing her long ago. Who knew? But he did realize he didn't want her to leave, at least not yet. They had the beginnings of something that felt so right. If only he could persuade her of that.

Zoey sent a text to Izzy to be sure she had the all-clear to depart for Banff tomorrow morning once her car was fixed.

"You still good with me staying at your place?" she typed.

"Oh, hey, Zo. Um, the thing is, well, yeah, you could go. I mean you're welcome to go."

"But?"

"But I think you'd hate me if you did. I don't know if I told you, but it's a one-bedroom. So you'd be on the sofa, and well, to be honest, I kind of think it might cramp our style if you know what I mean."

Zoey had an idea what she meant. If she and Tanner were in a one-bedroom cabin together, whoever slept on the sofa would be privy to far more than they'd ever want to hear. Might even scar them for life. But crap. That left her without a next stop on her "going nowhere fast" tour and facing the reality that she didn't have a plan. Maybe Bristol had been her Banff, and she'd already had her getaway. Complete with amazing sex and almost even better companionship, not to mention emotional healing. Maybe she needed to start figuring out what she wanted to do with herself. Go back to LA? Find somewhere new to settle? She hated making decisions. If only she knew what the fortune-teller had told Tanner. Maybe that would guide her. As soon as she was done texting Izzy, she would demand to know what Madame Whatever Her Name Was had told Tanner. At least then she'd know which direction to aim her car as she left the happiest time she'd experienced in ages in her rearview mirror.

It made her sad to think about that.

"Have you done it on a horse yet?" Izzy said, with a big laughing-face emoji.

"That's not on the camp schedule for today. Maybe tomorrow, but I'm heading out of here by then."

"Have you thought about staying? Sounds like you've enjoyed yourself."

Zoey tapped out an eye-roll emoji. "That would be weird. Like 'Hey, mind if I move in?'"

"Well, you don't have to move in with the guy. You can find a place to stay and see if you like the area and maybe start over. You and he can continue with whatever it is that you're doing, see where it takes you. You don't have to be his bitch or anything."

Zoey thought about that. She could stick around for the hell of it. Maybe by the end of the weekend, the convention would leave town and she could find an Airbnb to rent for a month or so. She didn't want to impose herself on Tanner. Perhaps they could continue with this thing, because, well, it *had* been crazy good. And she was sad thinking about how much fun they'd had together, not to mention the sexual connection between them. It seemed crazy to walk away from that.

"Maybe you're right." Zoey sighed. "In the meantime, hope you and Mr. HR have hot monkey sex all over the sofa since I won't be there to be skeeved out about it."

Tanner had fixed a farewell dinner of pasta puttanesca and a salad, using all fresh ingredients they'd bought at the market. He'd opened a bottle of Sangiovese, and when Zoey came into the kitchen, he handed her a glass.

"Wow, Tanner, this looks amazing. Anything I can do to help out?"

He shook his head. "Grab your wineglass and I'll bring everything out to the table."

He set the table on the back deck with a sunny yellow tablecloth and bright, colorful Italian dishes.

"This looks incredible!"

"For an incredible woman," he said with a wink.

He served her pasta and salad and then sat down and helped himself.

"So, Zoey, I've been thinking…" He steepled his fingers in front of him, elbows resting on the table.

"Me too, Tanner," she said, squinting at him.

"Oh. Okay…Well, by all means, you go first."

"No, it's fine, you can."

"I insist, ladies first."

Zoey frowned, took a deep breath, and let it out.

"So, it's time I found out what Madame Whoever She Is said about my future. Because I need some direction. I was going to head up to Banff to stay at my friend's cabin, but now I'm not welcome because she's going to be having hot monkey sex with the guy from HR, and now I don't even know what I should do. Izzy thought I should stay here in Bristol because I've enjoyed it, but honestly, Tanner, I don't want to be in your space. I mean, I've had an insanely good time with you the past couple of days, but I think we both recognize it's been a whirlwind. And while we kind of know each other in a weird way, there's so much we don't know about each other. The last thing I want to do is drop into your town and move in like some crazy stalker. I was thinking as soon as the weekend is up, I could find someplace to stay, and I could stay away from you, avoid you altogether and stay completely out of your space and enjoy the town, maybe do some hiking, that sort of thing. I would try hard not to bother you, but then maybe we could, like, you know, get together if the spirit moved us, and—"

Tanner held out his hands as he laughed. "I'm not completely sure I know what you're saying—"

She shook her head. "I was getting to that," she said. "Because before I decide what I'm going to do, I need to know what that woman said about my future. That way I know if I'm making the right decision."

Tanner opened his eyes wide. "So, let me get this straight." He took a sip of his wine, trying to figure out how to play this. "You're going to make a decision about the next step in your life based on what some supposed fortune-teller told you at a farmers market?"

She frowned. "Well, when you say it like that it sounds particularly crazy."

He nodded. "Ya think?"

Tears filled her eyes. "But Tanner, I'm terribly confused. I mean you've got me confused. And I've got me confused. I've found myself falling for you. Kinda hard. And it seems so damned impulsive and I was avoiding impulsive, remember? So that's a bad thing. And I was also getting far away from my previous life because I needed something new, remember that too? And I thought new was Banff, but then this happened." She spread her arms out around her. "And this." She pointed at him and then at herself. "And I don't know. I mean I don't know what to do. So I thought Madame Zazu or whatever her name is could give me some guidance."

Tanner reached across the table for her hand. "Why not trust your gut?"

"Well, I trust my gut. But I don't know what your gut wants, and I don't want to be rude if your gut disagrees with mine."

"Honey, I trust your gut implicitly."

"You do?"

He nodded. "Look, Zo. I haven't known how to say what I wanted to say, either. Because, well, it's nuts. We hardly know each other. I mean we know each other, and we knew each other, but you know. There's a lot to be known still."

"Right? Which is where Madame Zulu comes in. What did she say?"

Tanner swallowed hard. "I haven't wanted to say anything because I didn't want you to feel somehow obligated. But now it seems like maybe I was wrong in holding back."

"Well cough it up, would ya?" She grinned. "As long as it doesn't have me dying from the bubonic plague."

"I'm gonna go out on a limb and tell you that you're safe from that fate. Plague-free, even." He speared a forkful of pasta. "So here was the life prediction imparted from Madame Zorza: she said something old in your life is

121

something new. She said that fear would become trust. And she said that a big change was on the horizon."

She knit her brow. "And you're being honest with me? You're not making this up?"

He crossed his heart. "I swear to God. I mean, I was a little freaked out when she said all of this. Particularly when she said you would have ten children."

Her eyes opened wide. She took a large swig of her water. "That woman is so full of shit."

He laughed, clinking glasses with her. "Sorry, I can't tell a lie. That was my little fiction I added on."

Zoey wiped her brow in relief. "Oh, thank God. The rest of it sounds intriguing. The ten babies? Not so much."

Tanner leaned in, both forearms on the table. "In all seriousness, Zoey, this thing between us is fresh and new and who knows where it might go. But I'm interested in exploring that if you are. Why don't you stick around for a while, take a little vacation, see what you think about Bristol. And about me. And maybe see what Snowball thinks about Suki. We'd love to have you here. For a whole lot of reasons." He winked at her.

And it was then that it hit him: he'd been looking for home all these years and here it was, right under his nose, only he hadn't known it until now. Or maybe it took growing up and fleeing his original home that allowed him to find his true home. His gut was telling him a message loud and clear: there was a good chance that Zoey—and Snowball—would become a more permanent part of his life as well.

Thank you so much for reading *Skirt Chaser!* I hope you enjoyed it! If so, please help others find this book:

1. Help other people find this book by writing a review.

2. Sign up for my new releases email so you can find out about the next book as soon as it's available and get fun giveaways.
    http://eepurl.com/baaewn

3. Like my Facebook page.
    www.facebook.com/jennygardinerbooks

And I love to hear from readers! Let me know what you think about my books! You can write to me at jenny@jennygardiner.net, and visit me on the web at www.jennygardiner.net.

Keep reading for a sample from *Boy Toy*, the next book in the *Confessions of a Chick Magnet* series.

Boy Toy

By

Jenny Gardiner

Chapter One

SULLIVAN Forester stared into his underwear drawer for what seemed like the thousandth time over the past year, at the black velvet box nestled between the side of the drawer and a stack of boxers, topped by the pair with embroidered Saint Bernards on them. He shook his head, smacked his lips, then ran his fingers through his wavy caramel hair, which had gotten a little longer than he liked it of late. Finally he took a deep breath and blew it out, deciding once and for all to make it official: today was the day he was going to start getting his shit together, which included trimming this shaggy head of hair.

But first, he had more important business to attend to: the ring.

He pulled the box out of the drawer where it had lurked, taunting him for what seemed like ages now, and flipped open the lid to stare at the Tiffany & Co. two-carat brilliant-cut diamond engagement ring, flanked on either side by fat indigo-blue sapphires. The gems caught the early morning sunlight streaming through the window and winked at him. He took it as yet one more sign that it was time to find a new home for this thing that only felt like bad juju now that it had taken up unproductive space in his life for far too long.

At first, when Gretchen dumped him, three whoppingly inconsiderate weeks before their wedding, it felt like he would never get over it. Why would she do something like that to him? Worse still, how could he have been so clueless and not seen it coming?

A year ago, her words lacerated his heart, where he felt an achy tug that didn't seem to want to let go of him for months.

"Look, Sully," she'd said. "I just realized marriage isn't for me."

He remembered staring into her brown eyes, the ones that had once seemed so warm and loving, finally seeing them for the cold dark they really had been all along. Her hair had been pulled back into a high ponytail, her make-up fresh. She had on one of those bright pastel sundresses she always wore—what were they called? Lilly something or other. He knew dick about fashion, but he always noticed that she was about the only woman in town who dressed every day as if she was going to a cocktail party at a beach resort. He knew that style of dress only because in a way it was emblematic of what he'd left behind when he'd moved to Bristol, Montana a handful of years ago after selling his start-up for more money than he'd have ever imagined attached to his name—not to mention his bank account.

He'd spent a couple of years dabbling in the lavish me-me-me lifestyle of the very rich in New York: the obligatory summers in the Hamptons, the mandatory charity events every night of the week at somebody or other's exclusive penthouse apartment the rest of the year. The insincere air-kiss greetings by women who wanted your donations but not a decent conversation, the severe handshakes by the Wall Street assholes who were dipping into the cash reserves of the country to line their own pockets all while sticking their dicks into women young enough to be their daughters, as their air-kissing wives went under the knife for yet more unnecessary plastic surgery to try desperately to compete.

Sully was over that bullshit, which was why he'd come to Bristol. He wanted to start new where no one knew him, where he could be his authentic self and not play the superficial games to which he'd become accustomed.

His mistake, however, was bringing Gretchen Penobscott with him. He and Gretchen had been together even during the leaner years, so at least he could take comfort knowing it wasn't as if she'd been after his wealth. And to her credit, for a while, she went along with his plan, upending the lifestyle she'd become quite accustomed to. She came with him to Montana, Lilly whatever-the-name-was dresses and all, but it seemed from the minute they'd moved here, things never seemed quite the same between them.

He'd hoped it was just a matter of getting used to things—it was admittedly weird going from endless black pavement and skyscrapers to fields of wildflowers and mountains that touched the skies instead—and that once married she'd settle in more. But then he never got the chance to see if he was right, because on that brutal early summer day a year ago, she slid her ring off of her left ring finger, tucked it into the palm of his hand, closing his fingers around it, gave him a chaste kiss on the cheek, and walked away.

Well. He eventually learned that time does heal old wounds. And that while he once loved Gretchen, he realized she'd done him a solid by not going through with what she knew in her heart would be a mistake. He'd never really understand it, but hey, much better than finding that out after the wedding. Sure, it sucked, worse still having to take the financial hit for everything wedding-related he had to cancel last-minute, but the good news was it hadn't even put a dent in his bank account, so it was an emotionally costly but not financially detrimental lesson.

And today, he was going to take the first step toward making some other man who couldn't afford it that much happier.

He called for his Husky pup Blizzard, threw on a pair of shorts, a t-shirt, and a plaid flannel shirt to fend against the morning chill, grabbed his laptop and went out on the deck off of his bedroom. The sun was shining and the fog had just begun to lift off the still snow-capped mountain peaks as he fixed a quick cappuccino at the coffee bar he'd set up on his deck. He sat down at the long farmhouse table and opened his laptop, then snapped a quick picture of the ring on his phone, clicked on Facebook, then entered this:

Looking for a good home for this briefly used treasure, valued at $85,000. Tell me why you want to share this with the woman you love. Please email me at sully@sullyforester.com. Deadline is one week from today. Please share.

He uploaded the image, clicked "post" and sent it off into the ether, then did the same on Twitter and Instagram. He rubbed his hands together, took a sip of his cappuccino, and made a mental note to remember to stop in at Jackson's Barber Shop for a haircut when he went to town later on in the day.

Sully had been working on a song he'd been writing, reveling in the beautiful weather. It had started out chilly but by lunchtime it had become a quintessential Montana summer day: songbirds in full throat, the hum of bees vibrating through the air, all against the backdrop of a bluebird sky. Wildflowers were blooming like crazy in the fields surrounding his custom-built farmhouse that overlooked the Rocky Mountains. The place was truly a slice of heaven.

Life could not be any better. Sure, Sully didn't have a bride at his side as he'd originally expected, but it was all good. He'd gotten some regular gigs playing guitar at local bars, and that made him supremely happy making others happy with his music. He had a great dog that made him laugh with his antics. he got to spend time each morning doing what he wanted to do: reading, meditating, working out at the gym. He volunteered with an animal rescue clinic, thanks to his friend Tanner Eliasson, who was a local vet. He even spent an inordinate amount of time cooking elaborate meals for himself each night, which was admittedly a little lonely, and occasionally hosted dinners with a handful of folks who'd become true friends, not the superficial acquaintances he'd encountered regularly back on the East Coast.

Not to dig a jab at the East Coast—there was nothing wrong with that lifestyle for someone else; it just wasn't for him. He was happy on his horse, or feeding his chickens, or taking a hike on his hundred-acres of property. And more than happy to not have to deal with rush hour traffic and Type-A human beings ever again.

His phone buzzed and he pulled up a text message, from his friend Tanner:

Dude. What the fuck? Have you looked at your Facebook in the past hour?

Sully squinted, not knowing what exactly he was talking

about. Until he remembered.

Oh, that. You saw it?

He waited for the buzz of his phone.

Saw it? Me and a few thousand other complete strangers.

Sully's eyes opened wide. Huh?

You're joking, right?

Tanner didn't comment, but instead sent a screen shot of his post.

Sully expanded the image to see details up close. Holy shit. He grabbed his phone and pressed Tanner's number.

"Jesus, Sully," Tanner said. "Next time give me heads-up on these things. I've had every female I know within two hundred miles message me about this, and I didn't even know about it. You're *giving* away that ring?"

"I just figured it was time. The thing was just taking up space, reminding me of what was. No need in going there anymore. I'm finally past Gretchen, over that whole break-up, and I just want to make something that left a bad taste in my mouth become something better. Lemons to lemonade."

"That's a hell of a glass of lemonade," Tanner said.

"Yeah well, I thought it could be a fun project. And it would feel good helping someone else out who maybe couldn't afford to get engaged."

"Your fun project might turn into a full-time job if my suspicions are right—you're going to be slammed with people begging for that thing."

Sully shrugged. "Great! The good news is I've got time to do what I want. And right now this feels right. Besides, I'm sure I'll be able to see through the scammers looking for an expensive ring they could hock, and find someone who is truly in love and has a legit reason for wanting this thing. And to be honest, the sooner I get rid of this, it better. I want to move on without any reminders."

"Yeah, well, you'd better open up that laptop and start reading your emails because I think you've just given yourself a full-time unpaid job for the next year."

Sully laughed. "No worries. It's all good."

"Talk to me about 'all good' when you have a million women pounding your door down because they think you're the swooniest guy on the planet."

Huh. Sully hadn't thought about that. Shit. He sure as hell wasn't looking for women to glom on him for his money. Over the last year since Gretchen left, Sully had been in the habit of one-off flings with women tourists who streamed through Bristol like a hard-running river, looking for sporty outdoors activities by day and even more sporty activities in the sack by night. His music gigs offered the perfect opportunity to meet strangers in town for a short period of time, guaranteeing he could avoid anyone seeking commitment or anything more a few hours of escapist sex. He'd usually return with them to their hotel or Airbnb or rental up on the mountain, only to slip out hours later under cover of darkness, and be back in his own bed before sunrise. Sure it seemed impersonal, but that's what he'd needed at the time—anonymous sex for the sake of sex, no strings attached, no commitment whatsoever.

But now, crap, did this mean women were going to seek him out? He hadn't thought about that. He should've just donated the damned ring to charity, be done with it. Because the last thing he needed in his life was to have women honing in on him like a heat-seeking missile, wanting love and marriage and all those things he'd grown a bit cynical about.

He opened his Facebook page and saw that his post had been seen by three thousand people and had comments by over four hundred people. Hell, another two thousand had shared it. Ho-ly shit.

What had he gotten himself into?

Chapter Two

ISABELLE Strong was tired of licking her wounds over her latest failed relationship. Granted the hot guy from HR, her last impetuous fling, was never truly going to be long-term material—first off, nothing good came from dating a guy from the office. Secondly, it turned out he wasn't all that interesting. Once they got past the good sex—and she had to admit, it was good sex (the only reason it lasted as long as it did)—she found herself carrying most conversations while he spent an inordinate amount of time on the ESPN app of his phone. If he was going to be so deeply entrenched in his hand-held idiot device this early into a relationship, lord only knew how bad it would be after a few years together.

So she did what she knew she had to do, and lowered the boom, dumping HR-boy before things got any more involved. And now she really didn't miss him so much as the idea of him. Rather, the idea of a guy she could just have fun with, go away for the weekend, enjoy staying in to cook dinner with and maybe binge-watch several episodes of a show on Netflix before retiring for the night to stimulating sex, then falling asleep curled up in each others arms. Was that so much to ask for?

Apparently so. Because she'd had a succession of equally lame relationships over the past few years—from the lifeguard in Santa Monica whose idea of a good time was watching shark documentaries, to the waiter at The Ivy who only cared which famous celebrity he'd waited on that week. She had to lose him because she couldn't bear to hear one more time about how he'd yet again served lunch to one of the Kardashians. Then there was the weird guy who had the creepy toe fetish and insisted she wear sandals even when they went to Banff for the weekend to ski. In the winter. Uh, no.

She was stuck in traffic on the freeway and switched off her book tape and turned up the radio to try to find out what was causing the logjam on the highway. Instead she got the tail end of a news report about some guy who'd posted on Facebook about giving away a ridiculously expensive engagement ring to a deserving person, and that social networking sites had exploded over it. Huh. Intriguing. What sort of guy would have bought an eighty five thousand dollar engagement ring in the first place? And what self-respecting woman would ditch the kind of guy who did? Not that she was chasing after guys with money, but seriously, that woman must've been an idiot.

"The man, who lives in Bristol, Montana," the reporter said. "Is taking pleas from hopeful suitors until the end of the week."

Bristol, Montana? That was where her best friend Zoey Richards had moved to, after falling in love with a gorgeous veterinarian. She wondered if Zoey knew the guy. No time like the present to find out. She pulled out her phone to call her. Luckily Zoey answered on the first ring.

"What's shakin' bacon?" Zoey said in a half-whisper. "You are so not going to believe this but I'm sitting out back, sipping on my coffee, and all of a sudden I look off to my right, not a hundred and fifty feet from me, and see a moose. A moose! This place is amazing."

Izzy sighed. "Ugh. Don't be too jealous of me. I'm stuck

in traffic on the Santa Monica freeway, bored out of my mind, and just heard something on the radio about some guy in your town who's giving away a fancy engagement ring. What is up with that?" The traffic had slowed to a crawl so Izzy quickly pulled an elastic off her wrist and caught her hair in a ponytail, then put the phone back up to her ear.

"Yeah, crazy, right?"

"You know him?"

"Of course I do. In a town this size you get to know pretty much everyone. Especially with Tanner's line of work."

"So what's the deal?" Izzy saw a gap in the left lane and manipulated her car into it just as the driver laid on his horn and flipped her off. She reciprocated in kind. Damn, a girl could get repetitive stress disorder from flipping the finger while commuting in this town.

"He was engaged and she broke it off just before the wedding. It's been a year now and he's just ready to get rid of the ring—it felt like a bad luck thing to keep it. Not like he'd ever use it again anyhow."

"Shit I'd at least sell it. So he's just giving it away? That seems crazy."

"Believe me he doesn't need the money."

"Is he a nice guy?"

"He's great. Very chill. Laid back. Never heard a cross word out of his mouth."

"Great! I'm coming up to meet him." Izzy took the first exit she could and pulled over to program her Waze app to redirect her out of the traffic pileup.

"O-kayyyy... That seems a bit extreme," Zoey said. "But I'd be happy to see you regardless. You know you're always welcome."

"Perfect. I'm going home and packing a bag and driving

up there. I'll see you soon!"

Izzy always forgot what a long damned drive it was from L.A. to Bristol, a drive she'd done plenty of times since Zoey had transplanted herself there. It helped that it was right on the way to her place in Banff. But damn, she always felt like she'd been hit by a truck by the time she got there. It didn't help that instead of overnighting somewhere, she'd just pull over and sleep every couple of hours. A quick peek in the mirror revealed that her usually lustrous long, wavy dark hair looked like a fluffed-up dandelion on steroids. Her mascara, applied yesterday before she knew she was road-tripping that very day, had raccooned beneath her eyes in a most attractive way to make her look like a maniacal Victorian-era slasher. Her unbrushed teeth felt as if they'd sprouted fur. She was sure she was a sight for only the sorest of eyes.

She wanted to grab a token hostess gift to bring to Zoey and Tanner and figured a bottle of wine would suffice. She parked her car on Main Street and got out, walking the block or so to the wine shop, marveling as she did at the spectacular three hundred and sixty degree mountain views set against a pristine blue sky. Even the air felt amazing here, compared to the funk she breathed in regularly in L.A. She was so busy staring at the scenery that she failed to pay attention to where she was walking, and before she knew it she'd stepped in a disgusting, fresh pile of doggy doo. Furious, she looked around to see who was responsible for it, and just ahead of her she saw a guy with a plaid shirt over a t-shirt and pair of shorts demanding that a nearby husky puppy with bright blue eyes to come to him. The dog instead kept running circles around the sidewalk, defying his demands. He might as well have been flipping the finger at his owner, not to mention at Izzy and her mucked-up boots.

"You!" she said to the man, her voice rising higher the angrier she got thinking about it. All that crapola over her nice cowboy boots and now she had to get disgusting poop off of them before she could even get to Zoey and Tanner's.

The guy looked at her and pointed to himself, lifting a questioning brow.

"Yeah. You." She furrowed her forehead, then pointed at his pup. "Look what your damned dog did to me." She lifted her foot and showed him the smear on the sole of her boot.

The guy stopped walking and stared at her, eyes opened wide.

"My dog?" he shook his head vigorously. "How do you know that my dog did that?"

Izzy spread her arms out wide. "Um, do you see any other dog around?"

He frowned. "Not at this very minute, but that could have been left there hours ago by someone else's dog!"

"Not hardly," she said. "It's clearly freshly-laid. If that's a term. Ugh. I cannot believe I'm parsing out terminology for dog poop." She growled. "Look, dude. Curb your damned dog. You owe me a pair of boots. I just bought these things, too." She wagged her finger at him, as if that was going to achieve anything.

The guy approached her, his eyebrows knit, his lips pursed. "Quit your bitching, lady. My dog didn't do that. But if it's going to make you happy, here." He grabbed his wallet from his back pocket and pulled a handful of bills from within, reaching for her hand and stuffing them into her palm. "Now you can go out and buy yourself a new pair. Go crazy with it."

With that he turned away, whistled for his dog and muttered loud enough for Izzy to hear, "Let's go, Blizzard, and get away from the crazy lady before she hurts you." Then she saw him shake his head as he added, "Fucking tourists."

Izzy looked down at the money in her hand and realized he'd jammed six one hundred dollar bills there. Six hundred freaking dollars. In her hand. To replace her boots. That she'd gotten at TJ Maxx for about eighty bucks. Four years ago.

Well, that certainly was a best-case scenario for her boots, even if the guy was a bit of a jerk. She didn't have time to replace the footwear right now but with the cash in her hand, she removed the yucky one and dumped it in the trash can, limping the rest of the way back to her car, where she put on another pair of shoes till she got to Zoey's. What an inauspicious beginning to her quest to meet the charming ring donor. The good news was at least he wouldn't be a complete asshole like that guy was.

Boy Toy

Coming November 6, 2018

About the Author

Jenny Gardiner is the author of #1 Kindle Bestseller *Slim to None* and the award-winning novel *Sleeping with Ward Cleaver*. Her latest works are the *It's Reigning Men* series, the *Royal Romeos* series, the *Falling for Mr. Wrong* series and her new *Confessions of a Chick Magnet* series. She also published the memoir *Winging It: A Memoir of Caring for a Vengeful Parrot Who's Determined to Kill Me,* now re-titled *Bite Me: a Parrot, a Family and a Whole Lot of Flesh Wounds*; the novels *Anywhere but Here*, *Where the Heart Is*; the essay collection *Naked Man on Main Street*, and *Accidentally on Purpose* and *Compromising Positions* (writing as Erin Delany); and is a contributor to the humorous dog anthology *I'm Not the Biggest Bitch in This Relationship*.

Her work has been found in Ladies Home Journal, the Washington Post, Marie-Claire.com, and on NPR's Day to Day. She was also a columnist for Charlottesville's Daily Progress for over a decade, and is the Volunteer Coordinator for the Virginia Film Festival.

She has worked as a professional photographer, an orthodontic assistant (learning quite readily that she was not cut out for a career in polyester), a waitress (probably her highest-paying job), a TV reporter, a pre-obituary writer, as well as a publicist to a United States Senator (where she first learned to write fiction). She's photographed Prince Charles (and her assistant husband got him to chuckle!), Elizabeth Taylor, and the president of Uganda. She and her family and menagerie of pets now live a less exotic life in Virginia.

Visit Jenny at her website and sign up for her <u>newsletter</u>, her <u>blog</u>, or find her on <u>Facebook</u> and <u>Twitter</u>. And every blue moon she'll post adorable pictures of her pets on <u>Instagram</u> as @thejennygardiner.